MW00944143

The Angels
of Life and Death

ERIC BROWN

infinity plus

Copyright © 2010, 2012 Eric Brown

Cover © Dominic Harman

All rights reserved.

Published by infinity plus

www.infinityplus.co.uk/books

Follow @ipebooks on Twitter

First published in 2010 as an ebook by infinity plus.
This edition published in 2012, with additional story
"Seleema and the Spheretrix".

No portion of this book may be reproduced by any means, mechanical,
electronic, or otherwise, without first obtaining the permission of the
copyright holder.

The moral right of Eric Brown to be identified as the author of this
work has been asserted by him in accordance with the Copyright,
Designs and Patents Act of 1988.

ISBN: 1479242047

ISBN-13: 978-1479242047

BY THE SAME AUTHOR

Novels
The Devil's Nebula (Weird Space 1)
Helix Wars
The Kings of Eternity
Guardians of the Phoenix
Cosmopath
Xenopath
Necropath
Kéthani
Helix
New York Dreams
New York Blues
New York Nights
Penumbra
Engineman
Meridian Days

Novellas
Starship Winter
Gilbert and Edgar on Mars
Starship Fall
Revenge
Starship Summer
The Extraordinary Voyage of Jules Verne
Approaching Omega
A Writer's Life

Collections
Ghostwriting
Threshold Shift
The Fall of Tartarus
Deep Future
Parallax View (with Keith Brooke)
Blue Shifting
The Time-Lapsed Man

As Editor
The Mammoth Book of New Jules Verne Adventures
(with Mike Ashley)

CONTENTS

Introduction 9

Venus Macabre 11
The Frankenberg Process 25
Skyball 59
Bengal Blues 79
The Nilakantha Scream 99
The Thallian Intervention 121
The Tapestry of Time 135
The Frozen Woman 151
Crystals 165
Seleema and the Spheretrix 183
The Angels of Life and Death 203

Acknowledgements 217

About the Author 218
About the Cover Artist 218

More from infinity plus 219

INTRODUCTION

The received wisdom is that short story collections don't sell. Publishers are reluctant to put them out because, they say, readers don't want collections. And yet hundreds of collections are published every year, and hundreds of thousands of readers buy them. Perhaps what it is that publishers don't make as much money out of collections as they do from fat novels, as novels sell better than collections.

This collection brings together eleven of my tales dating from 1992 through to 2009. Some of the stories appeared in obscure, short-lived venues, while others came out in magazines without a wide distribution in either the UK or the US. They're collected here for the first time.

The first six stories are what I call core SF – stories set in the future (with one exception) and featuring the staple tropes of aliens, telepathy, star-travel, futuristic sports, etc. The last five tales are more contemporary and more character-oriented, while still rooted firmly in the science fiction genre. My favourite among them all is the title story, which pre-dates, and foreshadows, the Kéthani sequences of stories. An alien race comes to Earth bearing a gift from the stars...

Perhaps I should insert a word or two here about the type of science fiction I write. Or rather, perhaps, the type of SF I *don't* write. I don't write Hard SF. I have nothing against Hard SF.

(Well, perhaps I do – in my opinion it dates terribly, and if it isn't underpinned by decent characterisation then, in ten, twenty, thirty years' time, when the science is outmoded, it has little to commend it.) I write Soft SF, even Squishy SF; SF about how technology and science change people – and I like to think that I write about people. So the stories gathered here are principally about people, and plot, and *story* – that vital ingredient of the writer's craft.

The new edition of this collection contains the never-before-published story, "Seleema and the Spheretrix", which nearly saw print in an anthology, many years ago, but which never appeared. It was one of those stories which, once I'd finished it, cried out for more to be written about the characters and the setting. That was about five years ago now, and one day I hope to get round to writing more about the feisty Seleema and her love-interest, Mitch. It's a very light-hearted story on a serious subject.

My thanks to the editors of the magazines where these stories originally appeared and to Keith Brooke for allowing me the opportunity to assemble the tales under the aegis of Infinity Plus.

Eric Brown
Dunbar
East Lothian
2012

VENUS MACABRE

Devereaux chose Venus as the venue for his last public performance for two main reasons: the stars cannot be seen from the surface of the planet, and Venus is where he first died.

His performance parties are the event of the social calendar on whichever world he visits. The rich and famous are gathered tonight on the cantilevered patio of Manse Venusia, deep within the jungle of the southern continent: film stars and their young escorts, ambassadors and ministers of state, artists and big-name critics. They are all here, come to witness Jean-Philippe Devereaux perform what *Le Figaro* once described, before the Imams invoked the sharia on Earth and censored the reporting of such decadence, as *'an event of diabolical majesty!'*

Devereaux wears a white silk suit, Italian cut, long-lapelled. He moves from group to group with ease and grace. He converses knowledgeably with politicians and film stars, scientists and karque-hunters alike. His reputation as a polymath precedes him; intellectuals queue to fox him, in vain, with the latest conundrums of the age. He seems to have an intimate understanding of every philosophy and theory under the three hundred-and-counting suns of the Expansion.

Many guests, hoping that they might fathom the mystery of the man, find after a few minute's conversation that he is an enigma too deep to plumb. A paradox, also. He talks about everything, *everything*, but his art. The implication is that his art speaks for itself. Guests speculate that his pre-show ritual of socialisation – a bestowing upon them of his brilliance – is a ploy to point up the disparity between the urbanity of the man and the barbarity of his act, thereby commenting on the dichotomy inherent in the human condition. At least, this is the theory of those who have never before witnessed his performances. The guests who have followed his act from planet to planet around the Expansion know not to make such naive assumptions: his art is more complicated than that, they say, or alternatively more simple. One guest alone, beneath the arching crystal dome, speculates that his creations are nothing more than a catharsis, a blowing-out of the intense psychological pressures within his tortured psyche.

"By the way," Devereaux quips, almost as an afterthought, to each clique, "this will be my very last public performance."

He registers their surprise, their shock, and then the dawning realisation that they will witness tonight that pinnacle of performance arts, the ultimate act.

Devereaux moves from the marbled patio, up three steps to the bar. As he pours himself a cognac, he disengages from his Augmentation – that part of him he calls the Spider, which he employs in conversation with his guests – and descends to the biological. The descent is a merciful relief. He leaves behind the constant white noise of guilt which fills the Spider with despair. As he settles himself into his biological sensorium, he can tolerate the remorse: it simmers in his subconscious, emerging only occasionally in berserker fits of rage and self-loathing. He downs the cognac in one.

Devereaux turns to the guests gathered below and experiences a wave of hatred and disgust. He despises their ignorance. More, he despises their lack of understanding, their easy acceptance that what he lays before them is the epitome of fine art. He tells himself that he should not submit to such anger. Their very presence, at one thousand units a head, more than subsidises the cost of his therapy.

Across the crowded patio he catches sight of a familiar figure, and wonders if *he* is the exception. He did not invite Daniel Carrington; he came as the friend of a guest. Carrington stands in conversation with a Terraform scientist. He is tall and dark-haired. The perfection of his face is marred by a deep scar which runs down his forehead, between his eyes, over the bridge of his nose and across his left cheek. He was attacked six months ago by an irate subscriber to Venus-Satellite Vid-Vision, on which he hosts the most watched, though at the same time most hated, prime-time show. Carrington films suicides in the act of taking their lives. He employs an empath to locate potential subjects, and a swoop-team of camera-people and engineers. He films the death and follows it up with an in-depth psychological profile of the individual's life and their reasons for ending it. Wherever he is in the Expansion, Devereaux makes a point of watching the show. There is no doubting Carrington's sincerity, his humanitarianism, and yet although the programme is watched by *everyone*, he is universally reviled: it is as if his viewers, needing to transfer their guilt at their voyeurism, find in Daniel Carrington an obvious scapegoat... When he was attacked last year, he chose not to have the evidence of his mutilation repaired. He wears his wounds as the ultimate exhibition of defiant iconography.

Devereaux thinks that Carrington might be the only person in all the Expansion capable of understanding him.

He lays his glass aside and claps his hands.

"Ladies and gentlemen, if you please. I beg your indulgence."

Faces stare up at him.

He begins by telling them the story of the benign dictator of Delta Pavonis III, who loved his people and whose people loved him; a man of wisdom, wit and charm, who was assassinated long before resurrection techniques became the plaything of the ultra-rich.

"Tonight you will witness the tragedy of his demise."

He leads them from the dome and out onto the deck of the split-level garden, into the balmy sub-tropical night. On the lower deck is a stage, and before it the holographic projection of a crowd. The guests look down on a scene long gone, something quaint and maybe even poignant in the odd architecture of the stage, the costumes and coiffures of the colonists.

Devereaux descends to the lower deck, walks among the spectral crowd. They respond, cheer him. Something has happened to his appearance. He no longer resembles Jean-Philippe Devereaux. Projectors have transformed him into the double of the dictator. He mounts the stage and begins a speech. He recounts the life of the dictator, his theories and ideals.

The social elite of Venus watch, entranced.

Devereaux gestures.

Seconds before he is flayed alive in the laser crossfire, he sees Daniel Carrington staring down at him in appalled fascination. Then all is light as a dozen laser bolts find their target.

Purely as visual effect, his demise is beautiful to behold. His body is struck by the first laser; it drills his chest, turning him sideways. The second strikes laterally into his ribcage, compensating the turn and giving his already dying body the twitching vitality of a marionette. Then a dozen other bolts slam into him, taking the meat from his bones in a spectacular ejection of flesh and blood. For a fraction of a second, though it seems longer to the spectators, his skull remains suspended in mid-air – grotesquely connected to his flayed spinal cord – before it falls and rolls away.

Then darkness, silence.

After an initial pause, a period during which they are too shocked and stricken to move, the guests return inside. They are quiet, speaking barely in whispers as they try to evaluate the merit of the performance as a work of art.

On the darkened deck below, the hired surgeons and their minions are conscientiously gathering together Devereaux's remains. Hovering vacuums inhale his atomised body fluids; robot-drones collect the shards of bone and flaps of flesh. His skull has come to rest in one corner, grinning inanely.

From the circular orbit of the left eye socket, a silver ovoid the size of a swan's egg slowly emerges. A polished dome shows first, then pauses. Next, a long, jointed leg pulls itself free of the constriction, then another and another, until all eight are extricated. The Spider stands, straddling the ivory, grinning skull. Devereaux, with a three hundred and sixty degree view of the surrounding deck and the salvage work going on there, tests the Spider's spindly limbs one by one. When he has mastery of their movement, he hurries off towards the dome. The legs lift high and fast with an impression of mincing fastidiousness as he skitters through the bloody remains.

Locked within the digitised sensorium of the Spider, Devereaux is a prisoner of the guilt that suffuses the analogue of his mind. At least, when he inhabits his physical self, the guilt shunts itself off into the storage of his subconscious for long periods. The memory of his sins, his remorse and regret, have no refuge in the Spider: they are all up front, demanding attention. He cries out in silence for the refuge of his biological brain. He does not know how he will tolerate the next seven days, while the surgeons rebuild his body.

He scuttles up a ramp, through the garden and into the dome where the guests are gathered. A dozen of his spider-like toys scurry hither and yon, affording him the perfect cover.

He finds Carrington and climbs onto the back of an empty chair. He stands and watches, his body pulsing on the sprung suspension of his silver limbs.

"Perhaps," Carrington is saying, "rather than viewing his art from the standpoint of trying to work out what he *means*, what we should be asking ourselves is *why*? Why does he employ this macabre art form in the first place?"

There is silence around the table.

"Maybe," Carrington goes on, "the answer lies not so much in Devereaux's attempting to come to terms with the outside world, but with the monster that inhabits the darkness of his inner self."

Carrington turns his head and looks at the Spider, but his eyes do not dwell long enough for Devereaux to be sure if he knows for certain.

"I've heard it said that our host was once a starship pilot."

The Spider climbs down from the chair and skitters across the marble floor towards the darkness of the manse.

For Devereaux, the seven days he is captive in the Spider seem like as many years. Never has he known the time to pass so slowly. While he exists within the Spider he cannot sleep, nor shut down the process of intellection. The unbearable recollections from all those years ago howl without cessation in his awareness.

On the eighth day he is restored to his biological self. It is like coming home, returning to a familiar, comfortable domicile. He hurries to the lounge and checks his video and com for calls. There is a communiqué from Daniel Carrington. Will Devereaux care to meet him in Port City, to discuss a business proposal?

That evening, Devereaux sits in a leather armchair overlooking the jungle. He is aware of the degeneration of his body. He is exhausted. His bones ache. He is beset by irregular muscular spasms, hot and cold flushes and bouts nausea. This is to be expected. How many times has this body died, and been put back together again? Fifteen, twenty? Devereaux gives thanks that soon it will all be over. He looks ahead to his rendezvous with Carrington, the confession he will make to someone who will understand his guilt.

Devereaux hires a chauffeured air-car to transport him the five hundred kilometres to Port City. The metropolis has changed since his first visit to Venus, twenty years ago. Then it was little more than the beachhead settlement of an infant colony, struggling for autonomy from Earth. Now it is a thriving community the size of Tokyo or Rio, grown rich from the mining of the planet's many natural resources.

The air-car descends and speeds through the twilight streets to the headquarters of VenuSat, the station with which Carrington has his show.

He takes an elevator to the penthouse suite. A servant shows him along a corridor and into a large, glass-enclosed room, more like a greenhouse than a lounge, filled with a riot of brilliant blooms and vines. A white grand piano occupies an area of carpeted floor before a view of the illuminated city. Black and white photographs stare at him from every wall. He recognises them as the late subjects of Carrington's shows.

Carrington himself, urbane in a black roll-neck jacket and tight leggings, emerges from behind a stand of cacti.

He smiles and takes Devereaux's hand.

"So pleased..." he murmurs. The livid, diagonal scar that bisects his face is wax-like in the dim lighting.

"I conducted a little wager with myself that you would be in touch," Devereaux says.

"I found your final performance..." Carrington pauses, searching for the right word "...fascinating. Would you care for a drink?" He moves to the bar and pours two generous cognacs.

"Of everyone present that night," Devereaux says, "your speculations came closest to the truth."

Carrington affects surprise – but it is just that, an affectation. "They did?"

"You saw through the charade of the so-called 'act' and realised that it was nothing more than a rather self-indulgent form of therapy."

Carrington makes a modest gesture, not owning to such insight.

"I presume," Devereaux goes on, "that you summoned me here to find out why, why for the past twenty years I have indulged in such psychotherapy?"

He suspects that Carrington is wary of coming right out and saying that he wishes to record his very last act. Devereaux has the reputation of a temperamental recluse, an artist who might not view kindly the trivialisation of his death on prime-time vidvision.

But why else did Carrington summon him, other than to secure the rights to his ultimate performance?

Carrington surprises him by saying, casually, "But I know why you have resorted to these acts."

"You do?" Devereaux walks to the wall-window and stares out at the scintillating city. Surely, even so celebrated a journalist as Daniel Carrington could not successfully investigate events so far away, so long ago?

He turns, facing Carrington. "Perhaps you would care to explain?"

"By all means," Carrington says. "First, Jean-Philippe Devereaux is a *non-de-plume*, the name you took when you began your performances."

"Bravo!"

"Please, hear me out. Your real name is Jacques Minot, born in Orleans, 2060. You trained at the Orly Institute in Paris, graduated with honours and joined the Chantilly Line as a co-pilot on the bigship *Voltaire's Revenge*."

Devereaux — for although Carrington is correct, he will be Devereaux to his dying day — hangs an exaggerated bow. "I applaud your investigative skills, M. Carrington." He is oddly disturbed by the extent of Carrington's knowledge. He wanted to confess to him, admittedly — but in his own time.

Carrington continues, "You served on the *Voltaire* for ten years, then twenty years ago you were promoted to pilot and given your own 'ship, the *Pride of Bellatrix*. The same year you made the 'push to Janus, Aldebaran, and on the darkside of that planet something happened."

"But you don't know what?" He feels relief that Carrington does not know everything, that he will after all be able to confess.

"No, I do not know what happened," Carrington says. "But I know that it was enough to make you quit your job and perfect your bizarre art."

"I must applaud you. I never thought I would live to hear my past delineated with such clinical objectivity." He pauses. "But tell me — if you know nothing about what happened on Janus, how can you be so sure of my guilt?"

Carrington smiles, almost to himself. "You were a little insane when you landed on Venus all those years ago — perhaps you still are. You found a street kid. You gave him your laser and a lot of creds and told him to burn a hole in your head. You told him that you deserved it. Not that he needed any justification — all he wanted was the cash. But he couldn't bring himself to laser your head. He put a hole in your heart instead, figuring it was all the same anyway — you'd be just as dead. Except it wasn't the same at all. When the medics found that you were carrying a pilot's Spider Augmentation and had the creds to pay for rehabilitation, they brought you back. After that..." Carrington shrugs. "I think you developed a taste for dying as a way of assuaging your conscience. You turned it into an art form and it paid for your resurrections."

Devereaux says, "I take it you found the boy?"

Carrington makes a non-committal gesture, as if to say that he cannot divulge his sources.

Outside, lightning zigzags from the dense cloudrace, filling the room with an actinic stutter. Seconds later a cannonade of thunder trundles overhead.

"How did you find out?" Devereaux asks. "About my past, about what I intend to do?"

"What *do* you intend, M. Devereaux?"

Carrington's attitude surprises him. What might he gain by feigning ignorance?

"Let me proposition you, M. Carrington. You can have the exclusive rights to my absolute suicide, if you will listen to my confession..." Such a *small* price to pay.

"Your suicide?"

"Not just another performance – this will be the real thing. I have played with death long enough to know that nothing but true extinction can pay for what I did. Or did you think I planned an ultimate *physical* suicide, and that I intended to live on in my Augmentation, immortal? Now that would be a living hell!"

But Daniel Carrington is shocked. He stares at Devereaux, slowly shaking his head.

"No..." he says. "No, I can't let you do that."

Devereaux is flustered. "But come, isn't that why you wanted to see me? To arrange to broadcast the ultimate event?"

From the inside of his roll-neck jacket, Carrington withdraws a pistol. It is a karque-hunter's dart gun. He holds it in both hands and levels it at Devereaux.

"Do you think for a minute that I like what I do, M. Devereaux?"

"Why, my dear man..."

"Do you think I enjoy living with death? Christ, everyone on the planet despises me. I have this..." he gestures to his scarred face "...as a continual reminder."

Devereaux tries to be placatory. He is non-plussed.

"You didn't want to meet me to ask my permission–?" he begins.

"I asked you here to kill you," Carrington smiles.

Devereaux is sardonic. "With that?" he says. "My dear man, you'll need more than a dart gun to destroy my Spider." He pauses, peering at him. "But why?" he whispers.

"I've hated you for so long, Devereaux," Carrington smiles. "Of course, I naturally assumed you were dead – but I still felt hatred."

"You...?" Devereaux says. He recalls the kid he picked up, all those years ago.

"I didn't realise you'd survived, you see," Carrington says. "All I could think about was that you'd used me to kill yourself." He pauses. "Then I saw your picture on the vid, read about your forthcoming trip to Venus – and I knew I needed revenge. I had to kill you."

He fires without warning. The bolt hits Devereaux in the chest and kills him instantly – kills, that is, the body, the meat, the biological entity that is Jean-Philippe Devereaux. As the body falls to the floor, Devereaux finds himself in the sensorium of his Spider.

"Monsieur Carrington..." His transistorised voice issues from his unmoving lips. "There is a laser in the inside pocket of my jacket. If you set it at maximum, it will despatch my Augmentation."

Carrington is standing over him, staring down.

"But first..." Devereaux pleads. "First, please, let me confess."

"No!"

Carrington steps forward, slips a small laser from his jacket.

"That..." the Spider says "...is hardly powerful enough."

"For the past five years I've dreamed of this moment."

"Please, my confession!"

"I dreamed of putting you to death, Devereaux – but that would be too good for you."

Devereaux screams a hideous, "No!"

Carrington lifts the laser and, with an expression of revulsion, fires and separates Devereaux's head from his shoulders. He grasps the a hank of hair and lifts the head. Dimly, thorough failing eyes, Devereaux makes out on Carrington's features an expression of supreme satisfaction. "That would be far, far too good for you."

Time passes...

Devereaux has known seven days as a prisoner in his Spider – in one case ten days – but always these periods were made tolerable by the knowledge that soon he would be returned to his body. Now there is no such knowledge. Upon killing him, Carrington bisected his head and fished out the Spider, bound his limbs and imprisoned him within a black velvet pouch, so that he did not have even the compensation of vision with which to distract his attention from the inevitable... He had only his memories, which returned him again and again to the darkside of Janus.

At spiraldown, his co-pilot had withdrawn from the net, left Devereaux – or Minot, as he was then – to oversee the simple docking procedure. Devereaux had disengaged from his Spider a fraction of a second too soon, forgetting that he was on the darkside of Janus, where icy, hurricane-force winds scoured the port. He had not been paying attention, had been looking forward to his leave instead. The Spider would have been able to save the ship – calculated the realignment co-ordinates pulsed from the control tower – but Devereaux had no hope of processing so much information in so short a time. The *Pride of Bellatrix* overshot the dock and exploded into the terminal building, incinerating a hundred port workers, as well as the ship's three hundred passengers, beyond any chance of resurrection...

Devereaux alone had survived.

His dreams are forever filled with the faces of the dead, their screams, and the unremitting stars of darkside illuminating a scene of carnage.

Devereaux calculates that one week has passed when Daniel Carrington unties the pouch and daylight floods in. He expects Carrington to have devised for him some eternal torture: he will entomb him in concrete and pitch him into the deep Venusian sea, or bury him alive in the wilderness of the central desert.

Carrington lifts him from the velvet pouch.

Devereaux makes out the turgid Venusian overcast, and then the expanse of an ocean far below. They are on a chromium catwalk which follows the peak of a volcanic ridge. This is a northern tourist resort; silver domes dot the forbidding grey mountain-side.

Carrington turns and walks along a promontory overlooking the sea. Devereaux knows, with terrible foresight, what Carrington has planned.

Carrington holds the Spider before his eyes. Devereaux tries to struggle, realises then with mounting panic that his legs have been removed. Even his only means of psychological release, a scream, is denied him.

"I've had a long time to think about what I should do with you," Carrington whispers. "At first I wanted to kill you."

Devereaux cries a silent: No! He knows now that Carrington will pitch him into the sea, and that he will remain there for ever, alone with his memories and his remorse. He tries to conceive of an eternity of such torture, but his mind baulks at the enormity of the prospect.

"And then, when you told me that you intended to kill yourself anyway, I decided that there was another way of punishing you."

No! Devereaux yells to himself.

Carrington is shaking his head.

"But to do that would be as great a crime as doing what I thought I had done to you, twenty years ago." He stares off into the distance, reliving the past. "Perhaps the only way I can cure myself, Devereaux, is by saving you – and the only way I can save you is by destroying you."

Carrington turns then and strides along the catwalk. Seconds later he is standing on a railed gallery, a fumarole brimming with molten lava to his left. To his right, the ocean surges.

"Which way?" Carrington says. "Left, or right?"

He smiles. "Oblivion, or eternal torment?"

Oh, oblivion! Devereaux cries to himself.

Carrington smiles. He is not a cruel man, despite what people think. With little ceremony, he hefts the remains of the Spider and pitches it from the gallery.

Devereaux gives thanks to Daniel Carrington as he tumbles through the air. The seconds seem to expand to fill aeons. He experiences a surge of relief, and for the very last time the pain of guilt.

Devereaux hits the lava, and the casing of the Spider melts in the molten stream, and then he feels nothing.

THE FRANKENBERG PROCESS

The Director was still being interviewed by Security, so Freeman was called to the planning office to oversee a minor change in the schematic of the stealth interceptor.

He checked the plans, going through the changes. From time to time, white-coated techs hurried across the room with softscreens for him to check and initial. One hour later he sat back and admired the interceptor on the screen. It reminded him of a starship.

A starship, he thought to himself, smiling: what a quaint notion.

A rumour had spread through the manufactory that morning: Director Ruskin was under suspicion of selling secrets to the Indians. Freeman found it hard to believe. Ruskin had been seen in the city's Shah Jehan Tandoori last week, where, the story had it, he'd passed secrets to an Indian official over spiced ginger tea and barfi.

Freeman swivelled in his seat and stared out at the countryside rolling away to the horizon. The contrast between the stark silver geometry of the manufactory and the unspoilt rural beauty could not be more marked. Britain had prospered under the Western Alliance for the past thirty years; indeed, the West had never known such times. TelMass had brought that about, aided by the new range of stealth fighters. How could

India and the Asian bloc compete with the Alliance? The Indians still explored the Out-there with slower-than-light ion-driven starships, rendered obsolete with the advent of TelMass.

So why would anyone of the West even consider dealing with the East?

Freeman stirred, uncomfortable. From time to time a tiny, insidious voice whispered the answer, and he tried not to listen.

The com chimed. The screen, set into the arm of the chair, flared. He was surprised to see the bloated, over-indulged face of General Carstairs staring out at him. The Government man wore a black, side-fastening suit. Freeman was struck by the thought that, so dressed, out of uniform, the General was hiding something.

"Freeman? If you'd care to meet me in the green office immediately."

Freeman nodded. "I'm on my way."

He left the operations room and paced the long, curving corridor around the manufactory to the admin centre.

General Carstairs sat behind an oval silver desk. Overweight and old-fashioned, the military man struck Freeman as out of place in Director Ruskin's swivel chair.

Ominous, he thought.

"Take a seat," Carstairs said.

Only as he sat down did Freeman see, seated in the corner of the room, a casually-dressed civil servant he recognised from the news broadcasts: Carstair's aide-de-camp, Richards.

The General nodded towards a com-screen on the desk. Freeman made out lines of text.

"I've been assessing your records, Freeman. I'm impressed. Five years of exemplary duty under Ruskin. You've learned a lot. Whenever you filled in for him, you did well."

He was happy with his post of assistant Director. He had never hankered after promotion, and everything that would entail...

He knew what was coming. And he knew, too, that the rumours he'd heard that morning had been far from groundless.

Carstairs said, "I want you to consider promotion. Directorship of the manufactory. Starting next week. Of course, a translation to Beta Hydri 5 would be a concomitant. We know you must have considered the likelihood that one day... Even so, I'll give you until tomorrow to think about it, talk it over with your wife. However" – and here Carstairs fixed him with an unflinching gaze – "acceptance of the promotion would be highly advisable. Any questions?"

He shook his head, a feeling very much like sickness in his stomach. "None."

For the first time, Richards spoke. "Very good, Mr Freeman. I advise you to download the recommended philosophical tracts, if you haven't already done so. Frankenberg's treatise on the process will help you get your head around the finer ethical points."

Freeman nodded. "I'll do that."

General Carstairs killed his desk-com. "Very well, that will be all. I'll see you here at noon tomorrow."

Freeman stood, nodded to the General, and left the room.

In a daze of disbelief he took the escalator to the concourse, and only as he alighted did he notice the crowd of admin workers gathered on the piazza. They were staring across the sunlit square at a sleek blue security van parked outside the Director's office.

As if on cue, two guards emerged through the double doors. Between them, attempting to maintain some semblance of dignity, strode Director Ruskin. He stared straight ahead, his expression fixed, his complexion ashen.

Freeman felt his stomach turn.

Soon, a news report would announce the accidental death of Director Ruskin. His funeral would be attended by close family only, and given minimal coverage. Not long after that, all record of the Director's ever being a part of the Western Alliance's extensive infrastructure would be expunged from the record books.

Soon, Director Benjamin Ruskin would never have existed.

A salutary warning, Freeman thought. He could not suppress, however, the sickening sensation that curdled in his gut as Ruskin was manhandled into the back of the security van and driven away at speed.

As he sat back and slipped the auto into self-drive, Freeman considered the implications of the promotion offer.

Parkland sped by. Cloudless sky. The occasional hamlet came and went in a flash of designer-quaint terracotta tiles and topiary. Freeman closed his eyes.

The opportunity of a new start. The thought beguiled, and at the same time unnerved him. He would have to read Frankenberg, as Richards had suggested. He had never been able to fully understand the philosophical intricacies of the Process.

He reached out and activated his com. He entered Hansen's code. The screen set into the dash flared, and seconds later Doug Hansen was smiling out at him. "Joe. It's been too long."

"Busy, Doug. You wouldn't believe it. You free?"

"Just finished the afternoon shift. Why not come over? I'll be in the office."

The TelMass station soared high above the vales of rural Warwickshire in a classical series of scimitar sweeps. Atop the tripod, on the deck of the derrick itself, the control rooms were silhouetted against the afternoon sunlight like the superstructure of a battleship.

Freeman rode the elevator up the side of the station and walked down carpeted corridors to the manager's office overlooking the translation pad.

Doug had coffee brewed and poured. They sat on leather recliners before the floor-to-ceiling viewscreen and watched a team of technicians inspect the wiring beneath the deck plates.

"What do you fear?" Doug asked him, once Freeman had explained the situation. Trust Doug to cut to the quick!

"I don't know. I fear..." He sipped his coffee. "I fear staying here, I fear going."

Doug smiled. "Then you've nothing to fear," he said.

Doug Hansen had gone to Beta Hydri six months ago. Freeman was hoping for more than just platitudes from the man.

"What does it feel like?"

"Like nothing at all happened," the TelMass manager said. "Nothing at all. But, I admit, it is strange to think that out there..."

He stopped and stared at Freeman. "How is it between you and Emma?"

Freeman shrugged. He kept his gaze on the deck. "You know, when you love someone who doesn't love you... sometimes I don't know what I feel. For so long I've told myself that I do love her, hoping that some day she might change, say she loves me again." He shook his head. "I must admit, I've been thinking about a new start, a new life. I'd miss her, but how can you keep on loving someone who doesn't love you?"

Doug shook his head. In his eyes, Freeman could see an infinite sympathy. Doug's own marriage was damned near perfect.

"Joe, would Carstairs take no for an answer?"

"I could refuse, but I dread the consequences." He saw, in his mind's eye, the image of Ruskin being taken away by the security guards.

"Then you can't refuse. Go."

Freeman shook his head, near despair. "But what will it be like, Doug, to leave behind all I know, to start again on an alien world, a new life, with no going back?"

"Read your Frankenberg," Doug said, gently. He looked at his watch. "Dammit. I said I'd meet Caroline at five. Look, let's meet up tomorrow, okay? How about dinner at the Barn? Around six?"

They took the elevator to the parking lot, and Freeman watched the TelMass manager climb into his auto and speed onto the slip-road.

How can one be true to oneself under a totalitarian regime, he wondered?

There is no choice, when all free choice has been taken away by the dictates of central government. One cannot follow one's heart, because one's head knows full well the consequences. One is forced into doing what one is ordered to do – because to do otherwise would be considered insubordinate, and duly punished.

We are pawns, Freeman thought. Pawns pampered and cosseted, on a board of the finest mahogany, but pawns nonetheless.

We can but march relentlessly onward...

He'd heard that things were different in India and the other states of the East. Did Ruskin know something? Was that why he had taken the ultimate risk, and paid the price?

His auto drew into the drive of his villa. Emma would be home from school. How would she take what he had to tell her?

He felt an immense weariness settle over him as he climbed the steps and entered the lounge.

"You're late."

"I had to go over see Doug."

"Dinner's ready."

He followed her into the dining room.

She was small, slim, dark-haired, more attractive now in her late thirties than when he had met her five years ago.

She'd been married before and had a son, who split the week between Emma and her ex-husband in Warwick. Something about the fact that she was a mother – the centred, caring air it gave her – had immediately attracted Freeman. He had loved her from the outset, while in recent years she had showed him no more, it seemed, than grudging affection.

They ate in near silence, Freeman preoccupied with his thoughts.

Over coffee, she watched him above the rim of her cup. "What is it?"

He hesitated, wondering how she might take it. "I've been offered promotion."

Her eyes widened. "The Directorship? What happened to Ruskin? I thought he was there for life?"

He shook his head, shrugged, too sickened by what Ruskin had done to elucidate. "He was sacked. I don't know why."

She lowered her cup, staring at him. "Does it mean you'll be going off-planet?"

He nodded. "Beta Hydri 5."

Her jaw set as she tried to control her reaction. "I see. Of course, you could always refuse–"

"You don't understand. Refusal would be impossible. I'd be demoted, at least."

Her gaze was hard. "How do you think you'll manage? Alone, I mean. Without me?"

He shrugged. He dropped his gaze and let out a long sigh. "Emma, if our marriage was perfect... If you loved me, showed me affection from time to time–"

"You're such a romantic fool."

"I don't think it's too much to ask."

She pushed her cup aside, angry. "Your boss shouts, and you jump through the hoops."

"For Godsake, it isn't as if you'll be here alone."

"But you'll be there, Joe, without me."

He stared at her.

That was what this was about. She could not bear to think that he could live without her.

"I've had years of loving you and getting damn all back," he said. "You don't know what that does to someone."

He thought of an analogy. It was like working for the Government, working for a totalitarian regime, believing in it, until, finally, experience taught you that your belief was founded on nothing.

How could he tell her that?

"I thought you were satisfied with what we had," she began.

He knew that it would escalate into a shouting match, but he was saved by the chime of the house-com.

Emma jumped up and padded into the lounge. He heard her accept the call, a few indistinct words of the caller, and then his wife's strangled gasp, "Oh, my God!" followed by, "Joe... *Joe!*"

His stomach turning, he pushed himself from the table and almost ran into the lounge. Emma was kneeling on the floor, staring at the screen.

A face stared out, a woman's face made ugly by tears.

Caroline Hansen, Doug's wife.

Emma looked up at him, shaking her head. "It's Doug," she said. "Doug's dead. A road accident. Coming home. His auto-com malfunctioned and he ran into the back of a container-craft."

Freeman stared at Caroline. "We'll be right over, okay? We're on our way."

~

Doug and Caroline Hansen lived on a secure estate of mansion houses on the outskirts of Warwick. A militia van was parked outside the house. Two black-uniformed civil guards stood to attention beside the front door.

Freeman showed his ID card and pushed his way into the house.

Caroline sat on the settee, sobbing into a tissue. A policewoman sat beside her. When Emma ran to Caroline and took her in her arms, the policewoman stood and tactfully left the room.

While the women embraced, Freeman found himself looking around the room. Pictures of Doug and Caroline adorned the walls. The perfect couple. Freeman had never entered the lounge in the past without feeling a stab of involuntary jealousy at the good fortune of his friend.

He went in search of Scotch and found a half bottle behind the bar in the corner.

He poured three stiff measures. Emma forced the drink to Caroline's lips, and Freeman moved to the French window and stared out.

The sun was setting, reflecting off the lake that backed onto the mansions. A flight of mallard rose in a perfectly co-ordinated skein from the surface of the water, as if startled by the grieving woman's sobs.

Doug Hansen was an important man. A very important man. The government could not do without a TelMass manager of his calibre.

He considered the code of ethics laid down by Frankenberg in his writings. The scientist had suggested that a star-traveller should never return, for obvious reasons.

But, in the case of Doug Hansen, wouldn't it be different?

He wondered if such a case had occurred before in the five years since the initiation of TelMass travel.

He glanced back at the sobbing woman and cleared his throat. "Has General Carstairs been informed?"

Emma shot him a glance that said eloquently, *Not now, Joe!*

Caroline sniffed, shook her head. "The militia, they... they suggested he should be told. He's on his way over. To be honest, I don't really feel up to... If you could put him off."

Emma said, "Of course." She looked up at Freeman. "We'll take you back with us, Carrie."

Freeman heard a car draw up outside. He moved from the lounge, past the policewoman in the hall. When he opened the front door, General Carstairs and the ever-present Richards were striding up the path.

The general looked surprised. "Freeman?"

"My wife and I are friends of Doug and Caroline," he explained.

He showed the two men into the lounge. To his wife he said, "General Carstairs would like a little time alone with Caroline." He gestured his wife from the room.

She followed him into the adjacent kitchen. "At a time like this," she began as soon as they were out of earshot, "the last thing Carrie wants is the commiseration of some stuffed-shirt like..." She gestured towards the lounge.

Freeman ignored her. He stood by the window and stared out. The ducks were sweeping over the copse on the far side of the lake.

He wondered at the type of wildlife he might find on Beta Hydri 5. He had never bothered to access the documentaries about the planet. Perhaps, now, he would have to do a little research.

"Anyway," Emma was saying, "what does General whatever-his-name want with her? She needs to be with friends."

Five minutes later Freeman heard the sound of footsteps in the hall. The General and his aide were leaving.

Emma hurried into the lounge; Freeman followed.

Caroline was sitting upright on the sofa, slowly shaking her head as if in amazement. She smiled, radiantly, as Emma crossed the room and took her hand.

Freeman watched from the door.

"He's... he's coming back," Caroline managed. "General Carstairs said that rules are made to be broken. Can you believe that? Doug is coming back from Beta Hydri!"

That night, Freeman sat with a beer on the verandah of his villa and stared up at the mass of stars stretching across the heavens.

He pulled the softscreen onto his lap and called up the Frankenberg file. He read for fifteen minutes, but the convolutions of the complex logic defeated him.

He could understand the science behind the Frankenberg Process, but it was the idea underpinning the effect that had always left him baffled. Philosophers of every ilk and hue had tried to resolve the paradox, but never to his satisfaction. He supposed it would be a case of having to undergo the process himself, but even then he failed to see how he might come to understand what had eluded him for so long.

He accepted General Carstair's offer, of course, and the date of his departure was set for June 2nd, coincidentally the day of Doug Hansen's return from Beta Hydri.

On the evening of the 1st, he dined with Emma as if nothing untoward was about to take place. That night, in bed, she relented to his advances and allowed him to make love to her. It was like all the other occasions – a pleasure soon over, he inhibited in his passion by her evident reluctance to allow herself to let go, to give herself fully, to experience the pleasure that might have been possible.

In the morning she followed him out to the auto. He paused before slipping into the front seat.

"Goodbye," he said, meeting her gaze and attempting to read the emotions behind her eyes.

She reached out and touched his cheek. "Bye, Joe," she whispered.

"See you tonight," he said.

He drove away without a backward glance.

Freeman was strapped into the stasis frame on the deck of the TelMass derrick. He tensed as the countdown began. The medics had talked him through the process, explained some of the sensations he could be expected to undergo. He had read his Frankenberg over the course of the last few days. He knew full well what to expect.

But the theory could in no way prepare him for the fact.

"Three... two... one... *zero!*"

The word exploded in his head, along with the pain.

The pain... why hadn't they mentioned the pain? They had, of course – the medics had told him that he would experience a momentary burn as his physical self was shredded molecule by molecule and transmitted.

But no words could ready him for the absolute and exquisite agony that seemed to stretch for an eternity as he hung in the frame, head flung back, mouth torn open in a scream that issued from the depths of his soul.

And then it was over.

Oh, blessed cessation of all that was unholy.

A calm descended over his body, a balm. He was whole again, and without pain, and he felt cleansed, and made anew.

He was overcome with a sudden, insatiable curiosity. Where was he? He opened his eyes – and made out the TelMass derrick, the smiling faces of the technicians, and beyond them the rolling green hills of his beloved Warwickshire countryside.

Where was he? Where had he expected to be? He had known, all along, what to expect.

The Frankenberg Process.

He was examined by the medics, passed fit, and allowed home for the rest of the day before he took up the post of Director at the manufactory.

He left the TelMass station and dove home to Emma.

"Three... two... one... *zero!*"

The pain... why hadn't they mentioned the pain?

He hung in the frame, head flung back, and screamed out loud.

And then it was over.

A calm descended. He was whole again, and without pain. He felt cleansed, made anew.

He was overcome with a sudden, insatiable curiosity. Where was he? He opened his eyes – and made out the TelMass derrick, the smiling faces of technicians... but technicians new to him. Strangers.

He looked beyond the derrick and saw the alien landscape of Beta Hydri 5.

Where was he? Where had he expected to be? On beta Hydri 5, of course. He had known, all along, what to expect.

The Frankenberg Process.

The medics unfastened him from the stasis frame and led him across the deck to the recovery lounge. He stared about, in wonder, at the strange alien world that encroached on every side.

Would he ever become accustomed to so bizarre an environment?

He looked up, into the heavens, at the unfamiliar constellations in the dark sky overhead.

Somewhere out there, he knew, was Earth, and upon the Earth, as if nothing at all had happened, was one Joseph Freeman. But who was the copy, he asked himself, and who the original?

"Joe! Joe – it's great to see you!" He looked up. A familiar figure entered the room and hurried across to him, hand outstretched in greeting.

"Heard you were translating, Joe," Doug Hansen said. "Come on, I'll show you to your dome, give you a guided tour..."

They took a hanging mono-train to the residential domes, and Freeman sat and watched the alien world speed by outside.

He recalled the literature he'd read about the planet. Beta Hydri 5 – or Brightwell, named after the scientist who discovered it – was a jungle world. The colonists dwelled in a clearing filled with an agglomeration of domes like massed soap bubbles. The TelMass station occupied another clearing a kilometre away, linked by a mono-rail, and in the same clearing was the manufactory.

The trees were far taller than any variety found on Earth, and possessed great leaves which sprouted directly from their boles, confounding Freeman's image of what a tree should look like. And they were blue, or seemed to be in the twilight. From time to time deep booming sounds interrupted the smooth electric humming of the train. Doug explained that this was the mating call of the planet's dominant primate analogue.

Before he stepped from the carriage, Freeman pulled on the gloves Doug had given him, along with the face-mask.

There was oxygen in the atmosphere, but not sufficient to allow the colonists to go without the masks, which both supplied clean air and filtered out virulent spores harmful to the respiratory system.

Freeman followed Doug from the rail terminus along a suspended cat-walk through the jungle to his dome.

His new home was luxurious: a spacious lounge in the upper hemisphere, a bedroom and kitchen on the lower floor. At least the Alliance had spared no expense with accommodation, to compensate for the hostility of the planet beyond the wall of the dome.

Doug poured two drinks from a central bar and strode to the transparent membrane, staring out.

Freeman sat on a lounger with his brandy, still trying to come to terms with the fact of his translation.

Doug was leaner than when he had last seen him, a week ago on Earth. Of course, this was a different Doug to the one he'd known then. Or was it? No, it was the same Doug, but a different version. To think, just four days ago he'd attended Doug Hansen's funeral in Warwick.

He raised his hand and stared at it.

Doug turned from the wall, saw him and smiled.

"I know. Takes some getting used to."

"Who's the copy, Doug? I mean, is the Freeman back on Earth the original?"

Doug was shaking his head. "Haven't you read your Frankenberg? The dualist concept of copy and original breaks down in the process of translation. The subject is split, is the best way of describing it, and one remains on Earth while the other is flung... wherever."

Freeman took a shot of brandy. "How did you feel about going back, Doug, when you found out about the accident?"

"The Governor broke the news. He explained the situation, said they needed me back in Warwick. The thing was, I'd always missed Caroline and Earth. The pain at times was unbearable. I was excited by the prospect of returning to Caroline – of, from her point of view, returning from the dead."

"Even though you knew that another... another *you*... would remain here?"

"That's the paradox that even Frankenberg could never resolve, Joe." He smiled. "It's enough to know that I'm back on Earth, with Caroline. That she's not alone."

"But it can't ease the pain you must be experiencing now?"

Doug raised his glass. "We all make sacrifices, Joe. And what better sacrifices can one make than for the Alliance?"

Freeman stared into his drink, nodded finally.

He recalled Ruskin. "What happened to the Director, here?"

"Ruskin was removed from his post three days ago. I've only heard rumours from Earth. I was hoping you could fill me in."

"I heard he was secrets to the Indians. He was recruited just three months ago, apparently. Before that, he was a loyal Alliance man. It seems unfair that–"

"Unfair?"

Freeman looked up at Doug, standing tall and foursquare, glass in hand, beneath the curving wall of the dome.

"Ruskin came to Brightwell a year ago," Freeman said. "The Ruskin, here, is innocent of any crimes that the Ruskin on Earth committed. It seems harsh that he should pay for the sins of his Earth version."

Doug was shaking his head. "What you must remember, Joe, is that the Ruskin here can no longer be trusted. He's predisposed to treachery, by the very actions of his Earthbound-split."

"What happened to him? He wasn't–?"

Doug shook his head. "No. No, he was given some menial administrative post on the other side of the planet, well out of harm's way."

He moved to the bar and refilled the glasses. "Fill me in on Earth, Joe," he said. "How's Emma? How was Caroline the last time you saw her?"

They talked long into the night, as three huge moons climbed into the sky and illuminated the dome like searchlights.

Freeman took up his post two days later.

He socialised with Doug and his colleagues at the manufactory. The colony on Brightwell numbered some two thousand individuals, equivalent to the population of a small town on Earth. There were a few bars, a holo-vision cinerama, a sports complex.

From time to time Freeman took tours, in a sealed flier, to view the many wonders of the alien world, but always he returned to the safe familiarity of his dome with a feeling of relief.

He had been on Brightwell for a month when he realised that, not only did he miss Earth, but it was a nostalgia that would not be easily assuaged. There was no way that he might come to view this planet as home. It was too hostile and alien to senses and perceptions conditioned by almost forty years on Earth. There was nothing at all familiar about Brightwell. Even its name was a misnomer. The nights were long, the days short – six hours – and the quality of light during the day not bright at all, but aqueous. The trees bore no resemblance to trees on Earth, nor the wildlife – the specimens he'd come across were vicious, fanged things, like beasts from a nightmare. Even the flowers were spined and sickly-hued.

He missed the perfection of the sedate Warwickshire countryside. He wanted to step from the claustrophobic confines of the domes into fresh, clean air, without the encumbrance of face-masks or gloves. He missed the green hills and the blue skies of Earth, and the sense of history, the architecture that linked one subliminally with the past, that gave one a sense of connectedness he had altogether taken for granted. You only appreciate, he realised, what you have lost.

But most of all he missed Emma.

He missed the simple fact of her familiar humanity, the predictability of her ways. She was a good person, caring and humane. She might not have loved him – but she had felt some form of affection for him. And, anyway, what was love but a variable term applied to a concept that no one person could define absolutely?

As the weeks passed, he spent long hours after work alone in his dome, considering Emma and his lost life on Earth.

His job at the manufactory soon palled. He could delegate many of his duties, and when he was in the design office he often found his attention drifting.

He threw himself into the round of parties and social events with which the colonists attempted to amuse themselves. There was a soirée of some type or another every night, with imported spirits and locally fermented stuff in plentiful supply.

He met a number of single and attractive women, but the thought of initiating a relationship did not appeal. The image of Emma always intruded, reminding him of what he had left behind.

After a while, he discovered that there were others beside himself who were less than enamoured by life on Beta Hydri 5. Of course, on the surface, all appeared as it should: an industrious, loyal colony working hard for the betterment of the Alliance. But there was a constant sense of despair in the air. The colonists had the aspect of survivors of some apocalyptic accident, hanging on in desperation. Late at night, the parties winding down and alcohol having worked to loosen inhibitions, true feelings and sentiments were prone to make themselves known.

At one such party, in a dome by the edge of the clearing, he sat in a sunken sofa bunker with a woman in her twenties and finished off a bottle of gin.

He was aware of someone seated cross-legged on the floor, level with his head. It was Doug.

Freeman gestured drunkenly. "Doug, Doug, my good friend, Doug. Come and meet..." He peered at the woman. "What's your name?"

She smiled. "Susanna."

"Come and meet Susanna. She was saying – saying how she hated this hell-hole, Doug. I mean. Look at it!" He gestured through the wall of the dome at the monstrous forms of the bloated trees lowering over the settlement.

Doug joined them. He sat, legs outstretched, and regarded the glass balanced on his stomach.

"Actually, I didn't say hell-hole," Susanna said.

"But you meant it!" Freeman cried.

She laughed. "There are worse places, so I've heard. Groombridge 7 – what's it called? Can't remember. Anyway, it's supposed to be the pits."

He wondered if Susanna had changed the subject because she did not want to be seen to be criticising the Alliance.

He raised his glass. "If it's worse than this purgatory, then it must be bad."

Doug clapped a hand on his shoulder. "If you don't like it, why don't you request a move?"

A move? He'd had no idea that, having undergone one translation, another was possible. "A move? Request a move?" He hiccuped. "They'd allow that?"

Doug nodded. "So long as you've done a year here, and of course the move must be onward, to another colony world. You can't go back to Earth."

Freeman shook his head. "You can't go back to Earth..." he echoed drunkenly.

"Of course not," Susanna said, touching his leg. "The other you is there."

Freeman considered the other Joe Freeman, living his life, oblivious of Brightwell, in the rural idyll of Warwickshire. Did the bastard appreciate what he had, he wondered?

A move? He shook his head. "But it'd be no good!" he said, close to tears now. "I mean, I'd still be here, wouldn't I?"

Susanna smiled. "One of you would."

He peered into his glass, then looked up at Doug, who was staring at him. "I want to go back to Earth," he said. "I miss England. The beauty of the place... the sense of age, the things I took for granted when I was there, but can only appreciate now that I'm here. Christ, nostalgia is a terrible malady."

Later, Freeman thought back to the party and regretted his drunken honesty. What if some informer had overheard his woeful lament? The place was crawling with despicable yes-men, ready to denounce colleagues to curry favour and advance themselves.

A week later, Doug Hansen appeared at the manufactory just as Freeman's shift was ending. The sun was going down over the near horizon, but the three moons were rising: for the next four hours they would provide a magnesium half-light before the onset of the dark night proper.

Doug had hired a flier.

"I want to take you on a little trip," he explained as he escorted Freeman across to the vehicle. "Show you something."

They flew for two hours towards a range of central mountains, landing in the crumpled foothills where black water torrents tipped themselves like tongues of jet over cliffs of silver rock.

They stepped out beside an almost perfectly circular lagoon of sable water, like a brimming sink of crude oil, reflecting the bright light of the moons overhead.

Far away on the jungle horizon, Freeman made out the towering shape of the TelMass station, and beside it the manufactory.

"Beautiful," he said, "in its own way."

Doug had been quiet during the journey. Now he sat on an outcropping of rock and looked at Freeman through the tinted visor of his face-mask. Dressed from head to foot in scarlet coveralls, they appeared out of place in the alien landscape.

"What you said at that party the other week," he began, his voice muffled.

Freeman smiled. "Which party is that, exactly?" He had attended parties and dinners every night for months.

"You talked with Susanna and myself. About Brightwell."

For a terrible, heart-stopping moment, Freeman thought that Doug was about to tell him that his indiscretion had got back to the Governor.

"What about it?"

Doug stood and walked towards the edge of the drop, staring out across the jungle as it extended to the horizon.

"You said you wanted to go back to Earth."

Freeman hesitated. "That's right, I did."

"How do you feel now?"

Doug still had his back to him. The effect of talking to someone like this was unnerving.

It came to him that Doug might be an informer, one of the many government men set up to report on the sins of fellow workers.

He dismissed the thought. He'd known Doug Hansen for years. He was aware that he'd reddened, ashamed of the groundless suspicion.

"I... I still feel the same. I don't like it here. I made a mistake. Perhaps I should have remained on Earth, even if that would have meant losing my job." He shrugged. "Of course, I'm being wise after the event."

"But you still want to go back to Earth?"

Freeman smiled and kicked a shard of shale. "It's a futile dream, but one that's never far away."

His friend was silent for a time, then said, "It's possible, Joe."

At first, Freeman was sure that he'd misheard. "Excuse me?"

Doug turned and stared at him. "I said it's possible. It isn't a dream. It's possible to go back to Earth."

Freeman smiled. "Yes – if I die on Earth, you mean. That's the only way the authorities would allow it."

But Doug was shaking his head, and Freeman's heart commenced a loud and laboured beating.

"There's another way, Joe. A way of sending you back to Earth – the real you who's standing here now, not some split."

Freeman shook his head. "I don't see how..."

Doug sat down, cross-legged, on the black sand. Freeman joined him.

"I want to tell you something. This is between you and me, okay? If it ever got out..."

"You know you can trust me."

Doug nodded and released a long sigh. "Okay. The Frankenberg Process – the splitting of individuals at the moment of translation... Scientists working for the Alliance have made an important discovery."

For the life of him, Freeman could not imagine what the discovery might be.

"We've known about it for a year now. The big-wigs use it, Carstairs and the others, when they move back and forth between Earth and the colonies."

"Back up, Doug. You've lost me. What do you mean, use it?"

Doug said, "They use the TelMass process, the translation, without splitting. It's no longer a corollary of TelMass travel. You can go to your destination without somatic duplication, without leaving yourself behind. I've been overseeing the process, in secret, for nearly six months."

Freeman felt dizzy. He held his head in his hands, working through the implications of what Doug had told him.

"But why hasn't it been made public?"

Doug snorted a laugh. "Think about it, Joe! It benefits the Alliance to split its workforce, to have all its top men and women duplicated. It's cost-effective, and that's all the government thinks about."

Freeman stared at the scimitar shape of the TelMass station on the horizon.

He felt at once anger at the treachery of the Alliance, and a rapidly growing elation at the possibility...

"Doug, you mean it? You said I could go...?"

Doug licked his lips, nervous. "It's a risk. If we're caught... But I can do it. There's a consignment of cargo going off in three days, late at night. Once it arrives at Warwick, it'll be placed in storage before being unpacked. All you have to do is get out."

"Earth..." he said. Emma...

"The thing is, Joe, once you're there, you'll need a new identity. You'll be starting a new life, after all. You can't go back to how it was. You, a version of you, is still there."

Christ, Freeman thought, to meet oneself, to see oneself as others see us...

Doug was watching him. "You're aware of the risks? You still want to go through with it?"

"If you're prepared to risk it, Doug, then nothing can stop me." He paused, considering. "What about at this end, though? Won't they investigate my disappearance?"

"Hire a flier the day before you go. Program it to fly into the jungle and stay there, then meet me at the station. Let the authorities assume the rest."

For the next three days, Freeman had little thought for his work. He considered his return to Earth, what he might do upon his arrival. The thought of existing in a familiar landscape, of perhaps meeting Emma once again, filled him with elation.

Doug Hansen ensured the security were elsewhere that morning, and escorted Freeman across the deck.

He said goodbye to Doug, took one last look around at the jungle crowding in over the deck of the TelMass derrick, and stepped into the container.

Doug gripped his shoulder in farewell, then sealed the lid. Simple pressure from the inside would release the seal once the journey was over.

He crouched in the darkness, his heart labouring. He closed his eyes. He could see, as in the recurring dreams of Earth he'd been having lately, the green vales of England.

The container tipped, surprising him, as it was transported across the deck prior to translation.

Long seconds elapsed. Minutes.

The minutes stretched to what seemed like an hour, two.

Then he heard the countdown, and braced himself for the pain.

It tore through him, searing his every nerve ending. It was all he could do to stop himself from screaming out loud.

And then, as quickly as it began, the pain ceased.

He was on Earth... and no longer in pain. This was the start of his renewed life, his new beginning.

The container tipped. He was transported across the deck, tipped again, upright this time. Silence.

He would give it time, before unsealing the lid. Doug had explained that the containers were stored in a secure chamber for a day, before they were transported onwards. He'd given Freeman the exit code.

Ten minutes, he thought. Then he'd quit the chamber and take the service elevator to the parking lot. From there he could get a taxi into Warwick. He could withdraw sufficient funds from his account to set himself up in a new life somewhere.

He heard footsteps, shouted commands.

The container tipped. Light flooded in, blinding him, as the lid was forcibly removed.

Rough hands hauled him out. Security guards.

He was hauled to his feet and dragged from the container, aware only that this was the end. That there could be no salvation, now. He looked around him in disbelief, wanting to scream aloud in fear and desperation. He was not on Earth. Beyond the deck was the jungle of Beta Hydri 5.

But he had undergone translation, hadn't he? He had experienced the unmistakable, searing pain.

So what had happened?

And Doug? Oh, Jesus Christ...

Not only was he doomed – but Doug, too.

Then he looked across the deck towards the control room. Behind the long, rectangular viewscreen, two figures stood in silhouette. One was the Governor, the other Doug Hansen.

They were shaking hands.

As he was escorted across the deck between the guards, Freeman roared his rage at Doug's treachery, his lies.

Freeman heard the countdown and braced himself for the pain.

It tore through him, searing his every nerve ending. It was all he could do to stop himself screaming.

And then, as quickly as it began, the pain was gone.

He was on Earth... This was the start of his renewed life on Earth, his new beginning.

He heard footsteps ringing on the panels of the deck, and then shouts. "Start over here – we'll work through the consignment. They said he was concealed in a..." He lost the rest as the sound of his heartbeat deafened him.

He had been found out. Somehow, the authorities had discovered Doug's plan, notified the station personnel here.

He broke the seal on the lid and peered out. Half a dozen blue-uniformed security guards were moving across the deck, snapping the seals on containers identical to the one in which he was cowering.

Quickly he tipped the container and struggled free. In desperation he crawled across the deck and concealed himself behind a stack of crates. Beside him, on the deck, was an inspection cover. He lifted it and slipped inside, breathing more easily now that he was out of immediate danger. He pulled himself along the tight passage-way until he came to a downshaft, then climbed the ladder to the corridor and exited in the elevator.

As he left the station, he wondered how he had been found out, and if on Brightwell Doug Hansen was at this very second facing the terrible consequences...

He stared out of the taxi at the green fields slipping by outside. It was hard to believe that just fifteen minutes ago he had been on Brightwell, twenty light years away. Good God, but the beauty of the countryside was painful. He felt a stab of guilt as he considered Doug.

He instructed the driver to stop beside a cash-point on the outskirts of Warwick. He applied his palm to the dispenser and withdrew a thousand New Pounds, the maximum withdrawal allowable. It would set him up for a while.

He returned to the taxi, hesitated, and then gave the driver the address of his villa. There was the danger, of course, that security would send men to his house – but how could he began a new life in England without seeing Emma for one last time?

As the vehicle turned off the main road and approached the hamlet along the familiar, winding lane, Freeman thought of his wife and the new life he would have to lead without her.

This would be a hard goodbye, unlike the last one.

The taxi halted outside the villa. He paid the driver and approached the house. Only then, as he pushed through the gate, did he notice that his own auto was standing in the drive.

But by then it was too late to turn and run.

A figure moved behind the study window, and seconds later the front door opened.

The figure halted on the top step, staring at him in disbelief. Freeman swayed, dizzy. He was staring at himself, an identical copy of himself, and yet, though familiar, this Joseph Freeman before him possessed an aura of difference. It was, he realised later, merely that he was viewing himself in his entirety, a figure in the context of his environment, as he had never before seen himself.

Freeman raised a hand. "I can explain."

"My God," his double said, moving down the steps and approaching him along the path.

Realising that his double presented a danger, Freeman said, "We're the same, you and me. We need to work together."

"Jesus Christ, what happened?" His double was backing off, turning and running back into the villa.

If he contacted the authorities, warned Carstairs of what had happened... There was no way he could allow his double, in fright, to do that.

He gave chase.

The phone was in the kitchen, and that was where his double was heading.

Freeman sprinted after him, shouting, "Think about it! Listen to me..."

His double was already at the phone and frantically stabbing in the code. Freeman reached him and knocked the receiver from his grip.

"Listen to me!"

He looked into his own eyes, wide with fright, and did not like what he saw there. His fear, his cowardly reaction to the unknown.

His double backed towards a storage unit, and only when he reached behind him and pulled open the drawer did Freeman realise what he intended.

His double dived at him with a nine-inch carving knife.

Freeman parried the blow, then managed to grip his double's arm, the blade of the knife inches away from his chest.

In desperation, realising now that he was fighting for his life, he kneed his double in the crotch and forced the knife away from him.

His double lurched forward and, before Freeman could react, slipped on to the blade. It buried itself deep in his chest, and Freeman could only stare in horror as he – as his double – fell onto his back and stared at the ceiling, blood pumping from the wound and staining his white shirt.

Seconds later his double gasped, and his eyes glazed over, and Freeman fell to his knees beside the body and wept.

He looked up at the clock on the wall. It was three-thirty. Emma would be back at four.

How long had he been kneeling like this, sickened and disbelieving?

He had to move himself, get rid of the body.

He could always bury it in the garden – it would never be found: no one was looking for it, after all. But that would take time, and time he did not have.

He recalled his auto in the drive.

He tried to pick up the body, but was surprised by its weight. Instead of carrying the corpse, he grabbed the legs and dragged the body through the hall.

At the front door, he dropped the legs and hurried out to the auto. He opened the boot and checked the lane. There was no one about. He returned to the villa and manhandled the corpse through the door, wincing as its head cracked repeatedly against the stone steps.

With difficulty, he managed to lift the body into the boot. Exhausted, he slammed the cover and locked it, then returned to the villa.

There was a slick of blood on the kitchen floor, and a great arc across the wall. He mopped up, then moved to the hall and scrubbed the carpet. He showered and changed, wadding his old, blood-stained clothes into a plastic bag and stashing it with the corpse in the boot of the auto.

He returned to the villa, sat in the lounge and worked to calm himself.

No one need know anything about the events of the last few minutes. He would slip into his old life, blameless. There would be a gap in his memory of a few months, but he need not worry unduly about that. He would get by.

No one, after all, would suspect what had happened.

He heard the sound of an auto in the lane.

Emma, he thought.

It would have been a momentous event as it was, to meet his wife again after so long – but now he would have to face her knowing that he had, albeit accidentally, murdered her husband.

Thirty minutes ago, he told himself, I killed myself.

There was a knock at he door. But why would Emma bother knocking?

He left the lounge and moved to the hall. He made out two indistinct figures through the glass of the door.

He opened the door and stared. General Carstairs and his aide, Richards. He tried to remain calm. He reminded himself that he had nothing at all to worry about.

"Freeman," the General said. "We need to talk. Something rather untoward has cropped up."

His mind racing, Freeman showed the men into the lounge. They sat side by side on the sofa, refused a drink, and stared at him.

"Sit down," Carstairs said.

Trembling, he did so.

"This is a damned difficult situation, Freeman. Technically, of course, you're innocent."

"What happened?" he asked.

"Something occurred on Brightwell earlier today, an... indiscretion, let's say, involving yourself. That is, your Frankenberg-split. To cut a long story short, he managed to return to Earth illegally. We're doing all we can at this end to locate and arrest him."

He nodded, wondering how they had discovered Doug's plan in the first place.

He saw where this meeting was leading.

He gestured. "I don't see how this involves me."

"Technically, of course, you're not to blame. However, your Frankenberg-split did contravene Alliance edicts. He's under arrest on Brightwell as we speak, and of course can expect to suffer the consequences."

Freeman nodded, understanding suddenly hitting him like an unexpected upper-cut.

His Frankenberg-split was under arrest on Brightwell. Then everything Doug had told him...

There was no such thing as a one-way trip!

Doug had been lying, all along, in order to entrap him. The bastard was a loyal Alliance man, through and through.

The General was saying, "Such is the law that, in these situations, the innocent party must suffer certain consequences."

Freeman nodded. "I see." His pulse raced, and he realised that he was sweating. "What can I expect...?"

Carstairs waved. "No criminal proceedings, of course. But we will have to relieve you of your post as Director. Unfortunate, but the circumstances leave us with no other option. We'll find you some government admin post in town."

Freeman nodded, a sensation of relief sweeping through him. He would lead a reduced life-style, but he would have his freedom, and Emma.

"Of course," Richards was saying, "we'll have to requisition the house, as government property."

"Of course. I understand."

His visitors stood. General Carstairs nodded. "Very well, Freeman. I think that will be all for now. You'll need to appoint a lawyer. There'll be an official hearing in a month or so."

He showed the men to the door. They walked down the drive, past his auto, and stopped.

Carstairs and Richards spoke in hushed tones, glancing at the vehicle, and a hand closed around Freeman's heart, squeezing.

Carstairs returned to the front door.

"The auto is government property, too. If you could give Richards the key-card, he'll return it to the manufactory."

It was all Freeman could do to remain upright. He felt the blood drain from his face, and he could not find the words to protest.

He reached into his pocket for his key-card – but of course it was not there.

"Ah..." he found himself saying. "If I could possibly keep the car for an hour. You see, I pick up my wife from school around now. I could always drop the car back myself."

Carstairs returned to Richards. They conferred, and Freeman realised that his life depended on the General's next few words. He turned to Freeman.

"Very well," General Carstairs said, "but get it back by tonight, understood?"

"Perfectly, sir," Freeman said, and prayed that his wife would not choose that second to return.

He watched the men climb into their auto and move off down the lane.

Freeman sat in the lounge and considered his future. Short term, he would dispose of the body tonight, before returning the car. Long term... He considered his experiences, the treachery of the man he had once considered his best friend.

The terrible thing about living in a totalitarian state was that one could not be true to oneself... He saw again the fear in his double's eyes.

He knew a lot, he thought. What he could tell the so-called enemy about the top secret designs...

A minute later Emma steered her auto into the drive, and seconds after that she appeared in the doorway to the lounge. The sight of her, after so long, was shocking.

He stood, heart pounding. Emma approached him, reached up and kissed him on the cheek.

He put his hands on her shoulders, delaying her withdrawal. He could feel tears welling in his eyes.

He hugged her to him, relishing her warmth, her reality.

She pulled away from him and said, "Have I told you, Joe – ever since you left me, you... it's almost as if you've become a different person."

He felt a stab of insane jealousy, and smiled. "I don't think you've mentioned that, Emma."

She said, "You're more thoughtful, philosophical. Perhaps you've been considering the Process, what happened to you. And the other night, when you mentioned your doubts about what they did to Director Ruskin..."

"Yes?"

"Joe... for years I've wanted to hear you criticise the regime! I think I saw your compliance with the Alliance, and hated you for it."

He felt a welling of joy in his chest, and pulled her to him.

Emma changed the subject. "What's for dinner, Joe? I'm famished."

He considered what he had to tell her about his imminent demotion. He could do that over a meal.

"How about a take-away, Emma? I'll go fetch it now." He smiled. "I've heard the Shah Jehan is good."

The meal, he thought, would be the symbolic start of his imminent treachery.

She kissed him and moved to the bathroom.

Freeman left the house, climbed into his car, and drove from the house. The sun was going down, and a full moon rose insubstantial above the woods ahead.

He stopped in the track beside the lake, climbed out and stood in the dusk before opening the boot. He stared into the sky, at the stars appearing overhead, and realised that he was weeping tears of joy.

SKYBALL

I was in New Delhi the night the Tigers played the Cincinnati Raiders in the final of the World Skyball Championships. I would have made it anyway, but on the morning of the game Massingberd was tipped-off that some crazy was out for Cincinnati blood. He contacted me through my handset and downloaded all the data he had on sports assassins. Three hours later I stepped from the sub-orb in Delhi and booked into a two star hotel by the station – cheap enough to avoid being just another Western hotel transplanted East, but expensive enough to miss out on the piped dysentery that passed for water in some of the low-budget dives along the Paharganj. Around seven that night my deputy arrived. He lay on the bed and I clamped him into the stasis-brace. When I was satisfied that he was totally paralysed, I left the hotel and took an auto-rickshaw to the skyball stadium.

This was my first trip to India in ten years, and not much had changed. As we careered at breakneck speed through the crowded bazaars, narrowly missing barefoot pedestrians and roaming buffalo, I sat back and tried to ignore the filth and the poverty, the mutilated beggars and the families encamped in the gutters. In the night sky above the teeming streets, a floating newsscreen displayed images of an affluent, other world.

The venue for the final was the old Asian Games' stadium, extended with racked tiers when the Tigers gained promotion to the World League a decade ago. It dominated the flat Indian skyline like a floodlit mausoleum.

I paid off the driver and eased my way through the crowd. The atmosphere was electric. This was the first time the Tigers had reached the final and their opposition tonight were beset by injuries. The awareness that victory was by no means impossible supercharged the masses with an almost palpable optimism. Tiger pennants and banner-sized posters of Delhi high-attack and shield-strike heroes bobbed above a sea of eager faces: it was as if the Tigers had already lifted the cup.

I took the subway to the players' entrance, showed my pass at the door and stepped into the relative calm of the dressing rooms. Before I started work I wanted to look up Ed Harrow, the Raiders' player-coach and a friend from way back.

Ed was giving his team the usual pre-game pep-talk when I arrived. He passed from player to player with urgent, whispered advice, amicable jabs to red-shirted biceps – psychological tricks to assure each player they were the best and the opposition were a bunch of losers.

He was haranguing a bulky forward-strike when he looked up and saw me. He quit the lecture and strode over. He was a stocky, crew-cut bull of a man, a veteran of Nicaragua and for fifteen years the best skyball player the world had ever seen. He was getting old now, no longer the great he used to be; but he could still turn a mean shield and leave defenders for dead.

He grinned around the stump of a dead cigar. "Hey... What brings you here, Lou?"

"How could I miss the final, Ed?" I didn't want to spook him, so close to the game, with the real reason for my presence. We traded smalltalk.

I'd got to know Ed Harrow ten years ago, before I joined the Massingberd Agency. Then I'd used my talent in various ways – and one was to spot potential skyball players and pass them on to Ed. There was nothing to distinguish a good 'ball player from a bad one, physically. Skyball was fifty percent technology – with backpacks and shields and rebound bars – and fifty percent know-how. Anyone could be taught how to handle the technology, but only *special* people were able to grasp the game's logistics, the various stratagems and ploys that made a fair player a genius. As a transfer telepath, I could put myself in the minds of potential players and assess their worth. Over the years I'd supplied the Raiders with perhaps a dozen good players and three superstars.

Then Massingberd got hold of me and my days as a talent spotter were over.

I looked beyond Ed to the team, working out. Three full-backs shuttled a disc between their shields so fast it became a triangular blur. A couple of forwards backpacked to the ceiling and wrestled, the clash of pads loud in the confines. There was an air of grim determination in the room, unlike the usual confidence.

Ed sensed me pick up on it.

"Kent, Murray and Giraud are injured, and I'm playing like an old man. You see me last week?" I avoided his gaze. He'd missed three easy connections and had failed to collect a vital mid-space disc. "And the Tigers field a full-strength squad, unbeaten the last dozen games..." His hangdog expression said it all.

"You'll do it," I said, lamely. "I have a thousand on you to take the championship."

Ed grinned. "Sure we'll win, bud. Catch you later."

He returned to his players and laid into them with renewed vigour. I left the dressing room and took the tunnel towards the brilliant, floodlit playing area.

I came out on the third tier and the roar of the crowd hit me in a wave along with the sultry evening heat. One hundred thousand spectators were stacked in seven tiers around the mid-air court, a vast box demarcated by low-power lasers, like the three-dimensional diagram of an aquarium. At each end of the court was a goal board and, at strategic positions flanking the rectangle, padded rebound bars.

I stood at the top of the terracing and surveyed the crowd. Somewhere out there was the assassin – or perhaps not. Many death threats, especially those made against sports-stars and other celebrities, turned out to be hoaxes. But you could never be sure.

For the next hour, before the final began, I moved from level to level and speed-scanned hundreds of minds *en bloc*. I was looking for an anomaly, the psychotic cerebral signature of a killer. In seconds I could discount a thousand minds as mundane and harmless. I came across those that were far from harmless, of course, but none of these were planning to kill tonight. Their hatred was buried, latent, to emerge at some unknown, future date. It was the fiery beacon of the intentional killer that would guide me to him and bring about his arrest.

By the time the players filed from the tunnel, I was confident that the stadium was clean. I kept half a mind out for the late-comers who trickled in, then settled down to watch the game.

The New Delhi Tigers came out first to a thunderous roar from the home crowd, boosting themselves into the court and practising before the siren sounded. They vectored the magnetised disc from player to player, reversing the polarity of their shields to send the disc ricocheting away to a designated team member. They looked fast, confident: small men in the green and orange bodysuits of the Indian national flag. By contrast – as the opposition emerged to boos and cat-calls – the Raiders were giants in red, big and overweight. Appearances were deceptive, though. When so much depended on the technology of the booster, not much advantage was gained from stature. The Indians might be elusive in attack, but the Raiders had weight and power in defence. It would be a tough, even game – the advantage, if any, with the in-form home team. The crowd around me knew this and their cries were deafening.

I recognised Ed Harrow, floating belligerently in mid-space, small and squatter than the other Raiders as he hung from his backpack. He exhorted his team with a clenched fist and curses. The thirty players, gaudy in the floodlit court, waited anxiously for the start of the game. From his position on an air-scooter, the umpire activated the siren and tossed the disc. The crowd roared. The final was under way.

I made my way down to the lowest tier, to be near the street-level entrance and those fans still pushing through the turnstiles. I stood among a low-caste crowd, who could afford only the cheapest tickets, and watched the game progress above me.

The first third was a cautious affair, both teams afraid of over-extending themselves in attack in case they were caught by a rapid counter-move. The Tigers played their characteristic game: quick, fluid build ups, bouncing men from rebound bars as decoys as the legitimate attack came from either underneath or up-top. The Raiders replied stolidly, their slow attacks building from mid-space and pushing unimaginatively through the Tigers' central defence.

The Raiders scored first, against the run of play. A period of sustained Tigers' pressure came to nothing and the Cincinnati defence cleared a long disc quickly to a mid-spacer who supplied a forward with a deft short pass. The forward decoyed, lost his marker, and slipped the disc neatly into the top left corner of the goal board. A blanket silence greeted the move as the Raiders clashed shields and crashed helmets in celebration.

I read the resentment in the heads of the spectators, aware of the acrimonious stares directed at me, the only Westerner in the vicinity. Their disappointment was short-lived, though. With less than five minutes of the first third remaining, the home team equalised with a stunning long shot that left the Raider's defence floating impotently and casting around for someone to blame. The crowd's collective sense of relief was almost tangible. I kept my disappointment to myself and watched the celebrations. When the siren signalled the end of the third, I took the opportunity to scan fast, but there was nothing to worry about. I settled down to watch the second third.

As the period progressed, the Tigers stamped their authority on the game. They went three-one up and played like champions elect. The Cincinnati Raiders floundered, lost and unable to reply. I read Ed Harrow's mounting frustration as his team were pushed back into their own half and made to defend doggedly.

From time to time I cast around in the minds of the new arrivals who had taken advantage of the cheap tickets on sale halfway through the game. These people flooded in from the streets and jostled for a better view. I scanned repeatedly, but found nothing untoward.

Then, towards the end of the second third, I did come up with something interesting. The Tigers were four-two up and the crowd sensed victory. I rapidly entered a dozen minds and was about to exit when I recognised something in one of them. The kid – I couldn't see her for the press of humanity between us, but I stayed in their long enough to check her identity – was a born skyball player. I was taken back fifteen years, to the time when I worked for the Raiders. I'd found many a great ballplayer then, but none had initially hit me with as profound a knowledge of the game as possessed by this kid, Ananda Devi.

The final third began and I returned my attention to the game. The Tigers went five-two up, then the Raiders came back with two goals in as many minutes. With ten minutes to go the score stood at five-four, and the home crowd was frantic for the siren.

I think I was aware that Ed Harrow was having a poor game. He was marking badly and missing easy connections. It was hard to watch. Ed was a good friend, and no one likes to see a once great player, or a friend, embarrass himself.

But Ananda Devi knew. I found myself returning again and again to her mind. She gave the game total concentration and had the amazing facility to analyse and criticise moves already made, while at the same time assessing moves-in-progress and knowing, exactly and unerringly, where they should go. She had quickly realised that Ed was the weak link in the Raiders' mid-space structure, and knew where he was going wrong.

With one eye on the game I pushed my way through the packed spectators until I was standing beside the girl.

I knew already, having accessed her identity, that Ananda was a cripple; but the full horror and irony of the fact did not register until I saw her.

She was propped up in a home-made cart, an old fruit box with castors nailed to the corners. Some congenital disease had bequeathed her spine a cruel torque. Her legs were folded beneath her, thin and useless. She had the use of only one arm, the other hung limp across her soiled tee-shirt, which was printed with the legend Tiger, her nickname. She was either thirteen or fourteen – she didn't know which. Her parents had dumped her at birth.

And the tragedy was that in the West we had the surgical expertise to make Tiger fit and whole again.

Her rapt gaze on the game redirected my attention. I watched the final minutes of the contest through her eyes, her mind.

With a matter of seconds to go the Cincinnati Raiders fluked an equaliser. The Tigers failed to clear the disc in a goalmouth scramble and a Raider's high-attacker managed to squeeze a goal at the second attempt. I sensed Ananda's disappointment, but it was nothing beside her lingering despair at never being able to play the game she loved.

I hardly slept that night. I lay awake, thinking of Ananda Devi. When I did sleep, I dreamed I was inside her head, I experienced again the horror of her physical imprisonment. I awoke at dawn, dog-tired and sweating.

At ten I took an auto-rickshaw to where the Raiders were staying, a five-star hotel to the south of the city. There was a skyball court in the extensive grounds. The Raiders were in training when I arrived.

I wandered onto the court and watched Ed Harrow going through a strike stratagem with a couple of forwards. Despite his exhortations he seemed weary, as if last night's game had sapped his energy and enthusiasm. I felt a sudden surge of sympathy for Ed, then. I'd caught the reports on American satellite TV at breakfast. They were quick to condemn Harrow and his team for what they considered a poor performance.

As I watched the Raiders in practice, lulled by the regular clunk of disc on shield and the shouts of the players, I thought back a couple of years. I recalled a case I'd wrapped up in Amsterdam one summer. It was a straight transfer with my deputy as receiver, and it should have been an easy switch. I was chasing a killer who specialised in cops, and his cerebral signature stood out like a supernova. I traced him to a slouch bar in the port, moved in and made the transfer. But I fouled up bad somewhere along the line: I failed to establish my deputy securely in the head of the killer, and he had no control of the criminal's motor neurone system. Normally, my deputy would have walked the killer's body into the closest law enforcement station, and I would have made the return switch. Now the killer fled and I gave chase, desperately trying to get within range and complete the transfer.

I'd finally apprehended the killer aboard a crowded train, but for two hours I'd gone through mental torture holding the two identities in transfer simultaneously – and I'd vowed never to do it again.

Up in the court, Ed called a break. The players loafed around in the air, turning somersaults. Ed jetted down to where I sat, landed with a spurt of gravel and unbuckled his helmet.

He seemed exhausted and depressed and he smiled wearily as he sank down on the bench beside me. "Your thousand's still in there," he joked.

"I'm confident you'll do it," I told him.

"You are?" He grunted. "Things don't look too good to me, Lou. We played shit last night. We were lucky to get the draw. And you know something? The Tigers weren't on form, either. If they hit their stride in the replay..." he gestured, "we're dead meat."

"I don't know about that–" I began.

Ed shook his head. "God, I'd like to lift that Championship before I retire."

It was around noon, hot and humid. I was sweating and I'd done nothing to exert myself.

I said, "Listen, Ed... I've got this crazy idea. Bawl me out if you like, but I think I can help you."

Ed was about to laugh, then saw I was serious. "Yeah?"

"I can spot talent, right?"

"Like no on else. So?"

"So I read this kid last night who's a superstar."

Now he did laugh. "So you want me to sign him up, condense a year's training into a day and a half so I can field him in the replay on Saturday?"

"No, nothing like that, Ed. And the kid's not a he. She's a girl."

Ed gave me a look. "What you driving at?"

"While I was watching the game last night I accessed this kid. She's a cripple, but her understanding of the game is phenomenal. She knew exactly where the your team's strategy was fouling up and what you could do to put it right. She knew what you personally, Ed, were doing wrong. I know that if you'll allow me—"

Ed cut in, "Hey – okay, so we were bad. I admit it. But were we so bad that we'd improve with a cripple in the team?" He stopped then, stared at me, realisation hitting him late.

"You can't be serious?"

"Why not? I can do it. I can hold a transfer for ninety minutes, longer if need be..."

"Let's get this straight. You'd put the mind of this kid – this cripple – into one of my players for the duration of the replay, and you reckon she'd improve our game?"

"We've got two days to check it out, Ed. If all goes well, we play her. If not, then nothing's lost."

Ed was nodding to himself, staring at the ground. "Okay, so who do you suggest?" I sensed that he still couldn't quite bring himself to believe me. "Janovitch is off-form—"

I looked at him. "How about you, Ed?" I said.

He sat there for a while, unresponsive. He focused on a couple of players, shooting disc. At last he said, "So this kid's a genius, in theory. She's got it all up here. But what about all those potentials you sent me years ago? I admit they were good in theory, but in practice... I had to work them out for a year before they made the grade. How the hell do you hope to teach this cripple to use my body, and the equipment, in less than two days?"

I'd worked all that out on the way here.

"No problem, Ed. I'll transfer your mind into her head and vice versa, but I'll leave the part of you that controls your movement, the intuitive, instinctive motor neurone system. Her theoretical knowledge of the game and your empirical know-how will combine in one brilliant working part. It'll be hard on me, but I know I can do it."

"And just what do you get out of this?"

I smiled. "How much is it worth to have the Raiders lift the Championship?"

He calculated. "I'll give you a hundred thousand creds, if we win."

I nodded. "A hundred thou it is, then."

"But what about the kid? She's Indian, right? A Tigers' fan? You think she'll be willing to help the Raiders beat her team?"

"I think I know how I might persuade her," I told him.

"How soon can you contact her? You know where she lives?"

"I know where she sleeps. I'm going to see her tonight."

I held out my hand.

Warily, Ed shook it.

From the age of three until she was seven Ananda Devi lived in a tumbledown slum in Old Delhi, without the benefit of wheels. She existed by begging, stealing, and devouring the scraps and left-overs donated by generous food-stall owners. When she was seven, a Gujarati restaurateur built her a cart and gave her a charpoy outside his premises. She lived there now, on one full meal a day and whatever she could buy from the proceeds of begging in the busy Connaught Place.

The 'restaurant' was a lean-to wooden shack, identical to the dozen others erected beneath the towering outer wall of the Red Fort. All had battered cooking pots the size of small trash cans simmering on plinths of bricks, and tables and chairs outside.

Young boys in soiled vests and shorts hurried back and forth with trays and jugs of water.

I recognised Tiger's curry house from the rickety charpoy and her fruit-box cart parked beside it. Tiger herself sat at a table, thumbing through a skyball magazine and rapidly throwing rice into her mouth with her one good hand.

I sat down and ordered a meal. As I ate I sent a tentative probe towards Tiger. I confirmed the suspicion I had last night, that Tiger was an intelligent kid. In a way this was a tragedy – she might have been happier in ignorance. She was at that stage of adolescence when questions come naturally, and she was well aware of the fact that, had she been born in the West, surgery would have made her able-bodied.

She saw me staring at her and swung herself to the ground. Her legs, twisted equilaterals devoid of life, remained at right angles to her torso. She slumped into her cart and propelled herself across to my table. I thought reassurance at her, subliminally inviting her to join me. She grabbed the edge of the table and hoisted herself up. She was about to proffer a callused palm for baksheesh when some intimation of my purpose informed her otherwise.

Instead, she drew a connected-minds symbol in the dust on the table-top, and glanced up at me with big brown eyes.

"How do you know?" I asked, genuinely surprised.

"Last night, at game. I felt you in here." She pointed to her head.

"That's very perceptive of you, Ananda," I said patronisingly.

"Tiger," she corrected me. "What you want?"

"I read you last night, saw how much you understood the game. You realised how badly Ed Harrow was playing."

She regarded her fingers with downcast eyes.

I went on, "You thought you could play better than he was playing, if you had the chance."

The little girl shrugged.

"Do you know what a transfer telepath is, Tiger?"

Swiftly, she swung herself from the chair and accelerated her cart across the restaurant. For a second I thought I'd lost her. Then I read mounting excitement in her head, speculation.

From the charpoy she took a bundle of papers bound in a tee-shirt, her pillow during the night and portfolio at other times. She tossed the package onto the table, followed it up and rooted through assorted press-cuttings and glossy magazine photographs. She found a comic book and passed it to me.

I knew the magazine. It was a Hindi translation of a popular Western cartoon strip, featuring the exploits of a daring transfer telepath in the Out-there.

"Can you do that?" Tiger asked.

I nodded. "I can do that." I explained how I worked with my deputy to apprehend criminals.

"So?" She shrugged. "I don't understand." Though, of course, she did.

I said, "I want to put you into Ed Harrow's body for the replay on Saturday."

She took a while to respond. "Against the Tigers?" she asked in a diminutive voice.

I was relentless. "You'd be playing skyball for one of the world's greatest teams," I cajoled. "How would you like that?"

I saw myself reflected in her massive, staring eyes: an inverted Svengali promising the world.

She shook her head. "But I've never played before," she whispered.

So I told her what I'd told Ed earlier that day.

"Let me think!" she cried, near to tears, and shuttered her face behind a flattened palm.

"We'd make it worth your while, Tiger," I went on. "If you take Harrow's place in the team, and if the Raiders win, we'll take you back to the States. We'll straighten your spine and buy you a new arm and legs... Make you whole again, Tiger."

At eight the following morning Tiger trolleyed herself into the practice court. I was unable to tell whether her expression of grim resolution was due to the effort of propelling herself along like this, or the realisation of the treachery she was about to embark upon. I slipped into her mind and read a little of both. Soon, she hoped, she would be fit and mobile, and this means of transport would be a thing of the past; but the price of her resurrection was disloyalty to the team that had given her life so much meaning.

Last night I'd slipped her a hundred dollars, downpayment towards her full recovery. She had bought herself a new Tiger tee-shirt and a big Mickey Mouse watch.

Ed Harrow joined us, kitted-up and ready to go. He acknowledged Tiger with a brief nod, trying not to stare at her deformed body.

"Okay, so what now?" He was sweating, and I knew that he was nervous at the thought of the transfer.

"Boost yourself into the court, Ed. Take a few practice shots. I'll ease the transfer over a period of minutes."

Ed elbowed the rise-lever of his backpack and shot into the strike position at the far end of the court. The auto-server fired discs at him and he slammed them against the goal board.

"You ready, Tiger?"

She nodded, staring up at Harrow.

I closed my eyes and merged with the two separate identities. The process of transfer defies literal description. It's a cerebral, metaphysical discipline. The closest I can come to giving some idea of the sensation of the delicate process is to employ a metaphor: imagine juggling, one-handed, with egg yolks.

I accessed Ananda Devi and lifted her gently from the body she had known for thirteen years – at the same time taking Ed Harrow from his body and exchanging them, easing Ed into the prison of Tiger's twisted frame, and slipping a jubilant and ecstatic Tiger, incredulous that physicality could be so painless, into the super-fit body of the forty-five year-old pro-athlete.

I sagged back against the mesh fencing, exhausted from the transfer, and prepared myself for the sustained effort of maintaining the exchange.

My main concern, that Tiger's theoretical knowledge and Ed's practical skills would not mesh completely, was dispelled at once. Tiger, with a mental whoop of joy that rang wincingly inside my head, swooped on disc after disc and sent them bulleting remorselessly against the goal board. Within minutes she had full control of the body and, not content with straight shooting, sent herself bouncing from the rebound bars in tortuous rolls and jack-knives in time to intercept approaching discs and drive them home.

Beside me, Ed-in-Ananda stared up in disbelief. "She's a natural," he said, in Tiger's voice.

I held the transfer for ninety minutes, then let go. Ed and Tiger's identities snapped back into their respective heads, and I felt an immediate and sweeping relief. Ed lowered himself to the deck and joined us, exhausted after the work-out Tiger had put his body through. As for Tiger, she was breathless – not with exertion so much as the wonder of what she'd experienced.

"Again!" she demanded. "I want to play now!"

"I'm shattered, Tiger. Later, okay? This afternoon, when the other players are training."

Ed Harrow said, "The real test will be how you perform with the rest of the team, Tiger."

"I've been watching skyball for a long time, Mr Harrow."

I left them talking shop and went to the bar for a drink.

That afternoon, Ed set up a seven-a-side practice game. Seconds before the siren sounded, I made the transfer. For the next hour the body of Ed Harrow played vintage skyball. It was like watching the Harrow of old, the star strike who had thrilled crowds with daring stunts and virtuoso scoring feats. I sensed a stirring of renewed respect from his team-mates, who had begun to think that Ed had passed his best.

When the game finished and the players trooped from the court, I returned Ed and Tiger to their original bodies. Ed came across to us. "You played like a star, Ananda," he said in an undertone. "All set for tomorrow?"

Tiger avoided his gaze, looked away and nodded.

"Who's the kid, Ed?" a passing fullback laughed.

"Our new mascot." Ed tousled her hair. "Our good luck charm. Eh, Tiger?"

The following afternoon, before the replay, I transferred Ed and Tiger for one last work-out, and 'Harrow' played a cracker. He was on form again, just like the old days.

That evening there was a renewed sense of optimism in the Raiders' camp when we arrived at the dressing room. In contrast to the pre-match enthusiasm of the players, however, Tiger was quiet. I tried to reassure her that everything would turn out fine, but she just shrugged and pretended to concentrate on her skyball magazine.

When Ed led his team down the tunnel, towards the distant roar of the crowd, I tousled her hair. "Cheer up, Tiger. Think of your new future..." I probed, but there was so much conflict inside her head that all I got was mindmush.

I left her watching the pre-match commentary on the vid-screen and made my way to the stand. I found a seat on the fourth tier and prepared myself for the trauma of handling the transfer. Around me one hundred thousand zealous Tigers' supporters went wild as their team emerged and boosted themselves into the court.

I was about to begin the transfer when my hand began to tingle. I switched on, and Massingberd's big face filled my metacarpal screen.

"Massingberd?" I had the awful thought that he might need me on another case.

His expression was grim. "I just heard from the Cincinnati board of Directors, Lou–"

My heart skipped a beat. "And?"

"Someone contacted them five minutes ago. Get this – he's a Raiders' fan pissed at how the team's playing. He told the board that if the Raiders don't lift the championship he'll do something drastic."

"Christ..."

"Could be just another hoax, of course. But I'm glad you're there all the same. Good luck, Lou." He cut the connection.

It took a full minute for the implications to sink in.

Then I realised that the game was about to begin and I hadn't made the transfer. I closed my eyes, juggled Ed and Tiger's minds, and concentrated on keeping them where they were for the next ninety minutes.

There was no way I could maintain the transfer *and* scan for the potential assassin. I prayed that with Tiger's help the Raiders would win and 'disgruntled' from Cincinnati would have no reason to kill.

I could have aborted the transfer and scanned for the maniac. but the likelihood was that without Tiger's help the Raiders would go down: I would forfeit my hundred thousand, Ed would loose the championship and Tiger the opportunity of a new life...

Thus I persuaded myself that I was doing the right thing. Now it was up to Tiger.

The game was already twenty minutes old when I began to take an interest. 'Ed Harrow' was the dynamo of the Raiders' midfield, and before long the Tigers clamped two men on him and tried to shut him out of the game. This had the effect of giving 'Harrow' less of the play, but at the same time creating more openings for his team-mates. They took advantage of this, and when the siren blew for the end of the first third the Raiders were two-one up.

The second third began well, and despite the attention of two markers 'Harrow' played brilliantly. He frequently lost the defenders and made unstoppable flights for the goal board. He made the third goal and almost scored himself a minute later.

As the game progressed, though, the Tigers came back. They attacked the Raiders relentlessly, maintaining non-stop raids on the Cincinnati defence and effectively cutting 'Harrow' from the game. The crowd loved it – all the more when their team scored twice in five minutes to level the score at three-three with one thirty minute period to go.

I sat back and sweated it out, going through torture as I struggled to maintain the exchange. The constant mental effort of the past two days was beginning to have an effect. If the game had not been so evenly matched, I would have gladly returned Ed Harrow to the court. As it was, the presence of Tiger out there might easily decide the result.

It did – but not quite as I foresaw.

The third and final period was goalless until the last two minutes. 'Harrow' lost his markers and came back into the game, making neat vectors into opposition air-space, rebounding again and again to decoy defenders and in general playing like a star. At this stage of the contest it was 'Ed Harrow' versus the might of New Delhi. Behind me, vid-screen commentators were hailing it as the game of the decade.

Then, with a matter of seconds to go, 'Harrow' had the perfect opportunity to clinch the game for Cincinnati. He found himself alone in mid-space, with the Tiger's goal-stop hopelessly out of position. A long, accurate shot would have put the Raiders four-three up and given them the Championship.

Experts were still speculating a week later about what exactly was going through Ed Harrow's mind as he approached the goal board and played the shot that should have won the game.

The crowd fell silent as he came in to give the Raiders certain victory. He was alone and ten metres before the board, and the nearest Tigers' defender was another ten metres behind him. As the disc sailed in towards him from the wing, 'Harrow' raised his shield above his head to strike – and missed.

The crowd screamed as an Indian defender gathered the loose disc and slotted it through to an unmarked forward. The Indian triangle-passed with a second attacker, received the disc and scored with an ease that was almost arrogant. The stadium erupted.

As the siren sounded and the Tigers celebrated their first ever Championship, I gave up the transfer and returned Ed and Tiger to their respective selves.

Only then did I read the assassin, a focus of evil on the fifth tier. I stood up, frantically pushing through the celebrating crowd, desperately attempting to close the distance. I ran up the stairs to the next tier, aware of the killer in the crowd above me. I reached out with my mind to close him down, and for one searing second I experienced his psychosis. Then, before I could stop him, he fired.

I cried out in horror as I watched Ed spiral crazily through the air, his backpack mashed into the ruins of his chest, the centrifugal force of his rapid descent spraying blood in a great arc over terrified spectators.

Then, too late, I transferred the assassin...

I left the stand, ignoring the insistent tingle of my right hand as Massingberd attempted to get through. As I made my way to the dressing room, I realised then that I was crying, whether for myself, or for Ed or for Tiger, I had no idea.

I still wonder why Tiger missed that shot. I tried to probe her in the chaos that ensued, but her mind was a maelstrom of conflicting emotions. Was it the very fact that she had so much to gain that had preyed on her mind to the extent that she was unable to concentrate and score the winning goal? Or was it that she could not bring herself to be the instrument of the Tigers' downfall – that treachery towards the very thing that gave her life its meaning was not worth the reward of perfect health?

Whatever the reason, I could not find it in myself to blame her.

Nor could I blame her, really, for Ed Harrow's death.

I pushed through the swing door. There was no sign of Tiger – only a spilled skyball magazine on the floor and the vidscreen, relaying the horror to an empty room. I scanned, and read the unmistakable signal of Tiger's confused mind, burning bright, diminishing rapidly as she propelled herself through the crowded Delhi night.

BENGAL BLUES

Vaughan was three days into a routine murder investigation when the assassin came after him with a laser pistol.

The monsoon rains were late this year and it was another sultry day on Bengal Station. Any day now the seasonal downpour would drop unannounced from the heavens, deluging the top level and sluicing away the accumulated filth of months. Until then the heat would remain intolerable and the mood of the citizens increasingly fraught. The humidity incubated anger, and hair-trigger tempers tripped at the slightest provocation. Vaughan had been working for the Kapinsky Agency long enough to know that the crime rate spiked in the weeks leading up to the first rains. It was never his favourite time of year.

He sat at a table on the terrace of the Kit-Kat bar overlooking the vast sprawl of Bengal Station, the multi-level city-state situated in the Bay of Bengal between India and Burma. He touched the control of his wrist-pad, enabling his tele-ability, and instantly the minds of those around him flared into life.

Four days ago a high-class prostitute had been stabbed to death in an alley off Silom Road. The death of another working girl would have passed unnoticed, and uninvestigated, had she not been the favourite of someone high up in local government.

He'd talked to the girl's friends, and scanned them, but had come up with nothing.

Now he scanned at random, on the off chance that he might happen upon some stray thought, conscious or subconscious, that might lead him in the right direction. He flitted through minds close by, dipping for memories of the dead girl. She was known in the bar, but no one working or drinking here today knew anything about her death. The escort agency had its base next door, in the poly-carbon high rise that soared like a scimitar into the cloudless blue sky. Vaughan moved through the minds of the girls there, quickly, not wanting to mire himself in the short-term memories of working prostitutes: some had known the murder victim, and many were grieving. In a penthouse suite, Vaughan came across the pulsing collective signature of an orgy: a dozen Thai and Indian women and four high level Indian politicians were working up a sweat in the air-conditioned mattress-lined room reserved for gold-chip customers. One of the men was the dead girl's patron, sublimating his grief with the energetic assistance of his next favourite.

Vaughan withdrew his probe, despite the first stirrings of arousal – or perhaps because of them. In these situations, and in his line of work they were common, he felt like a voyeur.

He touched a control on his handset and mind-silence sealed over him. He wondered if it were guilt that moved him to dial Sukara's code.

"Jeff." His wife beamed up from his metacarpal screen. "How's it going?"

"Slowly. Are you at the hospital yet?"

"Daddy!" Li's round Thai face pushed Sukara from the frame and giggled at him. She looked better than she had for days, the waxy pallor gone from her face. "We going to see doctor!"

Sukara appeared again. "I'm just in the grounds. I'll call you when we've seen Dr Chang." She peered past him. "Are you in a bar, Mr Vaughan?"

He smiled. "All in the line of work."

She laughed and signed off. "Love you, Jeff."

It's something of nothing, he told himself for the hundredth time that day. Li had been sick for a week, listless and lacking appetite. He'd put it down to the time of year, but Sukara had taken Li to see their local medic who'd recommended a specialist, just to be on the safe side. Vaughan wished he'd been present at the examination, in order to read the truth behind the medic's bland platitudes.

He'd reassured Sukara that there was nothing to worry about, and wished he could convince himself.

"Mr Vaughan?"

He looked up. A gamin Thai street-kid, about fourteen, bandy-legged and flat-chested, squinted at him in the blazing sun.

He smiled. "How can I help?"

The girl made a nervous knot of her fingers. "Ah, you Sukara's husband, no?"

"That's right."

"You investigate murder of Kia, no?"

Vaughan sat up. "Right again. Why don't you sit down and I'll get you a drink?"

The kid winced as a flier screamed overhead. She slipped into the seat opposite and Vaughan ordered a mango lassi from a passing waiter. Her face was slick with sweat.

If the girl knew Sukara, then that meant she was a prostitute. Surreptitiously, below the level of the table, he enabled his tele-ability and for a second the girl's psyche swamped him.

He fielded the emanation, damped it down, and was surprised to learn that the kid was eighteen.

"You knew Kia, right?" he asked.

Her grief leapt at him. Images of Kia and the kid – her name was Lula – strolling through in the park were uppermost in her mind; deeper, and Vaughan saw the images of her every day work, the abuse she had suffered recently. He shut them out.

81

"Kia and me, we good friends. Like sisters. She knew man, regular customer. He frightened her, said he was going to kill her."

He probed, and the first thing he came across was the fact that she knew he was a telepath; she had debated coming to him with this information, at once not wanting him reading her secrets, but compelled to tell him what she knew.

And what pitiful secrets... She'd stolen a dress from the market last week, when she had no money; she'd enjoyed sex with a young man who treated her well... Vaughan felt a sudden upwelling of emotion and incipient tears stung his eyes.

She also knew what Sukara had told her: that she, Sukara, had once been a working girl, and now she was married to the finest man in the world. The kid thought it a fairy story, hardly believed it could be true, and Vaughan read in her juvenile mind the doubt that any relationship between a man and a woman could be as good as Sukara claimed.

"This man...?" he prompted.

He captured the image of the guy as it surfaced in her mind: a well-dressed Indian business-man.

"His name is Mr Narayan..." she began, but Vaughan already knew that, and more.

Narayan owned a plush sex club off Silom Road. He'd hired Kia's services once a week, then tried to lure her into working for him. When she'd refused, saying she didn't want to work with ee-tees, he'd beaten her and threatened her life.

The kid recounted all this to Vaughan between sips of lassi, and he nodded and let her go on. Whether Narayan was her killer remained to be seen, but it was his first lead in three days.

She faltered, then said, "Mr Vaughan...?"

He reached across the table and laid a hand on hers. "Kia wasn't in pain. It happened so quickly that she didn't even know she'd been attacked."

The girl's wide eyes leaked big tears and she bit her lip, nodding.

He was aware of her next question forming, and pre-empted it, "Of course I love Sukara. She's a very special person. We... we went through a lot together."

She said, "Maybe I'll find someone, one day, no?"

Vaughan nodded. "I think the boy you know, Ajay – he's a good person."

She beamed. "You think so? So do I!"

He read her joy as she stood up, making to go. Vaughan stopped her. He took out his wallet and offered her a hundred baht note.

She stared at the money, then murmured, "I don't want paying for telling you about Mr Narayan. I did it for Kia–"

"I think Kia would like you to buy the skirt you were looking at the other day. Didn't she always say you suited red?"

Lula smiled and took the note, then gave a quick wave and slipped from the terrace. Seconds later was lost in the crowd surging along the street.

He sipped his drink, leaving his tele-ability enabled; he was aware that the orgy next door had played itself out, the politicians returning to the senate while the girls took showers or counted their earnings.

He spoke into his handset and got through to a female-voiced computer program at the agency. "What can you tell me about a Mr Narayan, the owner of the Blue World bar, Silom Road?"

"One moment, please."

The reply came a second later. "Rajeesh Narayan, fifty-five, resident of Bengal Station, Indian national. Criminal record for illegal transference of cash, illicit narcotic substances. Residence: Penthouse suit, Blue World bar, Silom Road, Trat Mai sector."

"Anything else?" he asked.

"Negative."

He cut the link and looked along the street. The crowd surged down the thoroughfare like some multiheaded Chinese dragon, accompanied by a miasma of conflicting emotions. He was about to deactivate when he sensed something: a hundred metres to his left he came across an area of mind-static which indicated a citizen wearing a mind-shield. He looked up and caught a quick glimpse of someone staring his way. Seconds later the fluid movement of the crowd concealed the watcher.

He'd seen enough, though, to recognise the alien: a tall, jade-green humanoid from Tau Ceti III. What did they call themselves? The Korth.

He wondered at an ee-tee wearing a mind-shield. The fact was that the workings of alien minds were so abstruse as to be unreadable by human telepaths. He wondered if this one was taking no chances – or if he, Vaughan, was being paranoid. Had the alien actually been looking at him?

He scanned, but found no evidence of mind-static, and told himself not to be so uptight. The alien had evidently moved off, out of range.

He deactivated, relaxed into the resultant silence, and finished his drink.

Five minutes later he quit the terrace and slipped into the crowded street, making for the alley and Narayan's sex club.

Silom Road stretched from one corner of the Station to the other, a main arterial through-way connecting the rich Thai suburbs of the north-eastern sector with the spaceport. The raised railway ran parallel, along which white trains strobed like torpedoes; overhead, the din of the crowd was frequently drowned out by the scream of fliers criss-crossing the Station at five times the speed of sound.

He elbowed his way through the crowd. He was tall for a Westerner, and therefore a good head and shoulders taller than the Indians and Thais milling around him. He could see over the heads of the crowd to the near horizon, where skyscrapers and towerpiles bristled like the brandished weapons of a charging army.

He came to the alley and pushed his way through the crowd, then instinctively pressed himself against the crumbling wall and enabled his tele-ability.

He scanned, searching for the distinctive signature of mind-shield static. He thought he caught a brief signal – then it was gone, swept away in the surging pedestrian flow. He peered around the corner, looking for the tall jade-green Tau Cetian: all he saw were the familiar smiling faces of Thais and Indians going about their endless daily business. Reassured, but still wary enough to keep his program enabled, he moved off down the alley.

The Blue World bar was a discreet two-storey establishment – one floor on the top level of the Station, and the lower one on the level below – which fronted for an expensive and exclusive brothel.

As he flashed his ID at the surly doorman and pushed his way inside, Vaughan couldn't help being aware of the hundred or so minds within the bar. Half of them were human prostitutes, and in less than ten seconds he read everything from revulsion at the acts some of them were required to perform, to vicarious ecstasy at being made love to by the supernumerary phalluses of a Xerxean amphibian.

Then there were the alien minds, which communicated themselves to Vaughan as great abstract swirls of emotion, fragmented images he had no hope of decoding. He guessed it was something like being blind and having to make sense of an oil painting by dint of touch alone.

He steered his probes away from the alien miasma and looked for evidence of the bar's owner, Mr Narayan.

In the mind of a bar-girl he gleaned the information that Narayan would be returning at five. It was now just after three.

Vaughan moved to the bar, ordered a beer, then looked around the low-lighted room. The floor-space was divided into booths and areas of sunken sofas, where men and women entertained aliens with drinks and drugs before retiring to private rooms on the lower level. The walls were adorned with moving images of various worlds: he recognised the spaceport at Mars, the blue jungles of Jharu, Acrab II, and the famous floating cities of Gharab, Procyon VI.

His attention was snatched away by a new arrival in the entrance lobby to his left. He sensed the scratchy static of the mind-shield, then turned and saw the Tau Cetian slip into the room and move to a distant booth.

He counselled caution. There was no evidence, yet, to jump to the conclusion that the alien was following him. The bar was a legitimate destination for ee-tees, after all.

Then, in the mind of the bar-girl, he caught something. She'd seen the alien enter the bar, and the sight of it provoked a fleeting recollection. Vaughan read that yesterday she'd seen her boss, Mr Narayan, talking in hushed tones to the Korth in his office.

And the girl had overheard Narayan saying, "There's telepath on the case…"

Vaughan stood. "Where's the exit to Level Two?"

The girl gestured to the far end of the room and a darkened doorway. He pushed himself from the bar and hurried over to the exit.

Steps led down a stairwell. He descended, keeping tabs on the area of static in the bar above his head. He came to a second, smaller bar, around the perimeter of which were doors leading to bedrooms, group chambers and sex pools. Ahead was the sliding door of the exit, and beyond that the artificial daylight of Level Two.

He hurried towards the exit, pulse racing. Seconds later the static high above him shifted as the alien made its move.

The static moved towards him, then dropped as the alien took the stairwell.

He left the bar and crossed the concourse; the esplanades and outdoor bars were busy with citizens drawn to this level's air-conditioning, and the mind-noise was correspondingly loud. Vaughan damped it as he crossed towards the entrance of a municipal park, which called itself the Australasian Arboretum. Gum trees and eucalyptus extended for a kilometre in every direction, providing adequate cover from the pursuing Korth.

He entered the park and hurried along a path, rounded a bend, then ensuring he was unobserved stepped from the path and ducked through a stand of gum trees. He doubled back on himself, moving towards the concourse.

The Korth was on the second level now, pacing through the bar towards the exit. The hiss of static became louder in Vaughan's head as he came to the perimeter fence. He knelt, concealed himself behind a fan of ferns, and peered back towards the Blue World bar.

The alien emerged from the bar. Vaughan expected it to pause, assess its options before moving on. To his alarm, the Korth paced across the concourse towards the park's entrance. How the hell did it know? Unless, of course, it was guessing.

It wore a thick winter jacket – its homeworld was a sultry desert that made the Sahara seem like the north pole – and Vaughan knew that the bulky padding might easily conceal a weapon.

He considered his options, made a decision and moved. He ran through the vegetation that fringed the arboretum. There was another exit half a kay away; he'd take that and jump aboard a downchute to a crowded lower level, then attempt to lose himself there.

He probed. The alien was moving along the path. A second later it left the path and entered the shrubbery, heading towards him.

As Vaughan ran, he accessed his handset and got through to Kapinsky.

"Lin. I'm being followed. A Korth. Can you track me?"

She leaned to her right for a second, tapping a console. "I've got you on-screen."

"Get some security down here. I don't know how the bastard's doing it, but it knows where I am."

"You armed?"

"A laser. But I think the Korth's a professional assassin—"

"Shit. Okay..." She spoke into a throat-mic, summoning security, and Vaughan cut the connection.

He probed. The floating static was perhaps fifty metres to his right, moving straight through the undergrowth as the alien attempted to cut him off.

He pulled the laser from inside his shirt and thumbed off the safety control. He knew better than to bed down and enter into a shoot-out with the Korth. It probably packed far more fire-power than his standard issue laser pistol.

His only hope was to outrun the bastard until security caught up with him.

He heard what sounded like the roar of a flame-thrower, and a nano-second later a wall of vegetation to his right vaporised in an instant. His heart kicked. Reflex self-protection threw him to the ground as the broad beam of a laser sliced through the air where his torso had been. He rolled, fired instinctively, and saw the alien duck behind the shattered bole of a eucalyptus tree.

Vaughan dived for cover and crawled through a bed of loam, shouldering aside green bamboo shoots. He heard a second roar, heard foliage ignite behind him. He rolled onto his back and fired six times, hoping to buy himself time. He was about ten metres from the gate and the crowds that surged beyond. If he could lose himself in the press, make it to the downchute...

Then the alien called to him, and the sound sent fear tearing through Vaughan as the laser fire had failed to do.

"Vaughan." It was a high-pitched hiss, totally alien, sounding unlike any rendition of his name he'd heard before.

How in Christ's name was the bastard tracking him? Unless, of course, it was itself a telepath and was following the static of his own mind-shield. That had to be the answer.

If so, then once he made it to the crowd he could switch off his shield and his thoughts would be relatively indistinguishable among those of the citizens around him, especially as his pursuer was an ee-tee.

The idea gave him a kick of hope as he pulled himself through the last of the shrubbery before arriving at the gate.

He reckoned the Korth was around thirty metres behind him. He crouched, turned and laid down a burst of fire, then surged from the border and sprinted for the gate. A beam lashed after him, reducing the concrete gate-post to rubble.

Vaughan barged through the crowd, earning insults in three languages. He ducked his head and elbowed his way across the street, disabling his mind-shield and running a mantra he'd learned on a training course for just such a situation. The old Buddhist line, *Om mani padme hum...* Empty one's mind. Think of a flame, alone in the universe, then extinguish the flame, and think of nothing...

Which, with an alien assassin bent on slicing him into slivers, was easier said than done.

He probed. The Korth, signified by the area of static, had paused by the gate. The pause lasted three seconds, and then the alien was after him. At least, Vaughan thought, the bastard wouldn't fire through the crowd to get at him.

He was bigger than the citizens around him and, propelled by fear, he made rapid progress through the crowds to the gates of the drop-chute station. He sprinted towards the closing mesh gate of a carriage and barged his way in. The gate clanked shut behind him. He looked back through the diamond lattice as the carriage dropped ponderously. The signature static was ten metres away, though the alien itself was not visible through the press of humanity on the station concourse.

The carriage descended, leaving the second level behind, and Vaughan rationed himself to a small dose of relief.

He called Kapinsky. "Where the hell is security, Lin?"

"On their way. You're dropping from the second, right? The Korth is following in the next carriage. I have a team on the fourth level station. Get out there and lose yourself in the crowds."

"You got it."

He got through to the agency computer and said, "Korth, from Tau Ceti III. Are any of them telepathic?"

A fraction of a second later the soft female voice answered, "Not telepathic. Empathetic. They cannot reads thoughts, merely emotions."

"They can read the emotions of other species?"

"Affirmative," came the reply.

"And human mind-shields? Are they effective against the Korth?"

"Negative."

Which was how the Korth had tracked him so far, not by tracing the static given off by his integral mind-shield, but by identifying his emotional signature and locking onto it.

So much for being able to lose himself in a crowd...

He was pressed up against a fat Sikh and a bony sadhu, both eyeing the tall, sweating Westerner with bovine suspicion. It was hot in the overcrowded carriage and stank of rank body odour, but at least until the fourth level he was safe. After that, he would rely on the security team to earn their pay and save him.

He thought of Sukara, wondering why the sudden vision of her should enter his head now. She was smiling at him, giggling over a glass of wine...

A minute later the carriage slowed and bobbed to a halt. The mesh gate rattled open and Vaughan popped himself from the press.

He hurried through the station, attempting to work out who among the loitering citizens were members of the security team. He scanned, detected half a dozen mind-shields in the vicinity, and hoped they wouldn't stand on ceremony when the Korth emerged. He'd never before believed in summary execution, but there was nothing like the threat of death to encourage a shift of opinion.

He exited, looked left and right, and headed for an alleyway packed with Indians who were leaving a cinema.

Above him, the Korth was dropping towards Level Four. He kept probing as he was carried along in the flow of humanity. The static ceased its fall, was held in place – obviously as the carriage came to a halt and the gates opened – then it moved again, on a horizontal plane.

Seconds later the other mind-shields in the vicinity converged.

Even a hundred yards away Vaughan heard the shouts and screams, and the roar of the incendiary laser beam.

Sickened, he slid his probe around the station. Five of the six mind-shields belonging to security were still, unmoving. One was mobile, but had slowed significantly, and Vaughan guessed the man was injured and rolling in agony.

One area of mind-static had exited the station and was heading down the alley towards him.

The Korth, presumably.

If he could out-run the bastard, put about a half kilometre between him and his pursuer and get himself out of range of the alien's mind-probes, then he was home free... The problem was, how to do that among the press of humanity on this level? The rub was, he needed the crowd to give him some measure of cover and protection, but he needed relatively open space if he were to make a run for it...

Then he remembered the Aquaworld habitat on this level, and allowed himself a second small ration of hope.

He squeezed from the crowd, sprinted along a relatively depopulated boulevard, then cut across a plaza towards the beckoning logo of a leaping dolphin, above which arced the legend: Aquaworld.

A week back, after bringing Li and Pham here to sample the water-wonders of amazing Aquaworld, he'd vowed never again to be suckered into the crass black hole of corporate merchandising. Now he approached the gates as if they were the pearly portals of heaven itself.

He probed. The alien was in the alley, turning into the boulevard. About a hundred metres away, Vaughan estimated.

He ran through the entrance, throwing a wad of baht at a startled clerk, and headed towards the Antares IV waterworld concession.

Families lined up before the air-locks that gave access to the variously sized submersibles, but the lock for the one-man subs was vacant. He overpaid another clerk and slipped into the air-lock. Seconds later he inserted himself feet-first into the sub, dogged the hatch and steered through the irising portal. He accelerated and shot from the air-lock and into the facsimile of the aqueous habitat of Antares IV.

Last week he'd taken the girls on a leisurely tour of everything the vast tank had to offer, taking in the coral habitats of the squid-analogues and the great shoals of the planet's sentient natives, the diaphanous cetaceans who communicated via a complex sequencing of their polychromatic internal organs. Now he made straight for the diametrically opposite air-lock down on the fifth level. The tank was, he guessed, about a kilometre square; with luck he'd be able to out-run the limit of the Korth's mind-probe and lose himself in the crowds when he exited.

He sent out a probe. The patch of static was dimming as he drew away from the air-lock. He gripped the controls and shot between a shoal of tiny silver fish, like a million coins moving as one: these were the unique Sarth, he recalled, a sub-sentient hive-mind in control of a myriad separate bodies.

His handset buzzed. He accessed the call.

"Jeff," Kapinsky said, "Good thinking. We have teams on Levels Four and Five and tracking the Korth."

"Tell 'em to take care. You saw what the bastard did to the first team?"

"They're taking appropriate measures, Jeff. See you soon."

"Let's hope so," Vaughan replied, but Kapinsky had cut the link.

He probed again, and to his relief failed to locate the signature static. All he picked up was the mind-noise of the families flitting through the water in their subs, and the distant thoughts of individuals situated around the tank's near perimeter.

He looked ahead; he could see the vast wall of the tank, camouflaged with a multi-coloured coral effect, before which flitted shoals of alien fish. He sighted the circular hatch of an air-lock and headed for it.

A minute later he slipped his sub into the hatch. The vehicle rang as mechanical grabs made it fast and water sluiced from the lock. A green light indicated that it was safe for Vaughan to alight. He pushed himself from the sub and hurried to the outer hatch, shallow breathing to mitigate the stench of Antares brine and seaweed.

Second later he was through the hatch and striding towards the Aquaworld exit. He probed. There was no evidence of the mind-shield static in the vicinity.

This sector of Level Five was a business district, and the three-storey offices crammed between the level's floor and ceiling were emptying of tired citizens after a day's shift. Thankfully Vaughan joined them, inserting himself into a flow of Tata drones as they made for the nearest drop-chute station.

He continued past it and a few hundred metres further on slipped into a bar and ordered a Blue Mountain beer.

He regained his breath, and along with it his composure. In retrospect, he allowed himself to feel the fear that his adrenaline had so far kept at bay. With the delayed fear came the intellectual fall-out: for whatever reason, someone had set an alien assassin on his trail.

His thoughts were interrupted by the summons of his handset. That would be Kapinsky, to tell him that security had got the Korth and he was free to show his face.

He accessed the call.

"Sukara?"

She stared out at him. She looked, he thought, shocked. It came to him that she was aware, somehow, of what had happened to him. Then she spoke to him, and began weeping.

He listened to what she had to say, and it was as if something inside him had turned to ice.

He shook his head and asked her to tell him again, and she repeated herself. She said she'd see him back at the apartment in an hour and cut the connection.

Vaughan stared at the blank screen, his heartbeat thudding.

When he looked up, he saw the Korth standing in the entrance to the bar and scanning the drinkers in the bar's dim interior.

He should never have let Sukara's call divert his attention from probing for the mind-shield static. Then, he might have done something about the approach of the alien assassin. But it had cornered him, and instead of feeling fear, all he did feel was a sadness for Sukara and the girls if he failed to best the alien in the ensuing shoot-out.

He went for his laser, at the same time wondering why the Korth hadn't singled him out and attacked immediately. As he surreptitiously thumbed off the safety control, it came to him. The Korth was an empath, and had been locked onto his earlier emotional signature.

The fact was that Sukara's call had, briefly, disrupted that default signature, camouflaging it with his shock...

No sooner had this thought formulated than the alien turned, easing its laser from the folds of its padded jacket.

Something moved behind the Korth, and before either the alien or Vaughan had time to discharge their respective weapons, a woman in combat fatigues yelled something Vaughan didn't catch.

The alien pirouetted, levelling its laser, and the woman fired. The flash blinded Vaughan and he ducked. When he looked up, the Korth was swaying in the entrance, headless, before falling in stages on its multi-jointed legs, scattering tables and chairs.

Watched by petrified customers, the woman stepped over the alien's corpse, holstering her pistol, and strode over to Vaughan while the rest of her team moved in on the alien. She gave him a hostile look.

"Vaughan?"

He nodded.

"You're one lucky son of a bitch, man," she said.

"Lucky?" he whispered to himself as the woman rejoined her team.

He raised his wrist and activated his com, replaying Sukara's message. He stared at her grief-stricken face.

"Jeff," she had wept. "Jeff, I've just seen Dr Chang, and he said, he said…" She broke down, then managed, "Jeff, Li has leukaemia!"

Vaughan killed his handset, a hard pressure lodged in his chest.

He moved from the bar and took the upchute to Level One. He emerged from the station and looked up into the sky. Stormclouds were massing. The time was four forty-five.

He hurried along Silom Road, making for the Blue World bar. He turned down the alley, enabling his tele-ability and scanning ahead. He found the bar-girl he'd read earlier, and probed. Narayan had not yet arrived. He probed deeper, discovered which entrance the bar's owner would use.

He hurried along the alley and came to a private, recessed entrance. He stood with his back against the door, his heartbeat loud in his ears, and scanned.

Five minutes later he detected a patch of mind-static approaching along the alley. An Indian in his fifties turned into the entrance, stopping suddenly with a comical expression of surprise on his fat face.

Vaughan reached out, grabbed a handful of silk shirt, and punched the Indian hard. He went down, his nose shattered and blood spoiling his shirt. Vaughan kneeled over him and said, "Where's your shield?"

The Indian babbled in fear. "What?"

"Your shield?"

Narayan's eyes widened suddenly. "You! The telepath…"

If Narayan was shielded with an implanted cortical device, Vaughan would have no option but to take him into custody and have the authorities probe him.

But if his shield was not implanted...

Vaughan saw a chain about the man's fat neck, reached out and yanked.

"No!" Narayan yelled.

Vaughan smiled at the oval pendant on the chain. He tossed it into the alley and probed.

And the images he found in the cess-pit of the bar owner's mind confirmed his suspicions. He was rocked by the power of Narayan's anger as he beat up the prostitute, Kia; if only she hadn't fought back, then Narayan might not have drawn his knife, stabbed her repeatedly in the belly—

Vaughan quickly withdrew his probe.

Narayan stared up at him, petrified.

Smiling, Vaughan drew his laser and thumbed it to stun.

"No!" Narayan yelled.

"This is for Kia," he said, and gave the bastard a quick pulse in the head, curtailing his screams. He stood and got through to Lin.

"Jeff, you okay?"

"I've got the killer, Lin," he said. He gave her the co-ordinates.

"Well done, Jeff."

He cut the connection.

He looked down at Narayan. He'd be out for the next hour or so. He gripped the butt of his laser. What he'd like to do, what he'd really like to do, was thumb the laser to kill and fry the bastard.

But that was just his anger, his anger at what Narayan had done to Kia, his anger at being trailed by a Korth assassin. Even, he realised, his anger at the injustice that his daughter was ill.

Instead of killing Narayan, Vaughan stepped over the recumbent form and stood in the alley. It was what Sukara would have wanted him to do, after all.

He felt something on his head, and looked up into the sky.

The monsoon rains had begun.

THE NILAKANTHA SCREAM

Sabine is in Rio, checking out the stalls in the cryogen-mart for a retinal graft, when her hand tingles with an incoming call. Østergaart smiles up from her miniature metacarpal screen.

"What do you want?" Sabine says, surprised.

"I want to see you," her boss says. "The Historical Participatorium, Lisbon. Six hours." He smiles again and is gone.

This is the first time in years that Ø has contacted her himself, and the summons worries her. How often has she told him that she cannot return his love? Like everyone with riches and power, Ø assumes he can buy his every desire. He'd fallen in love with Sabine when he'd read her head ten years ago, had plucked her from the Antananarivo slum of her childhood and employed her in his agency. Years later, when she had grown, matured, he approached her with offers of marriage and fabulous wealth, but by then it was too late. So why the summons now? Hell, he had tele-ability – he could probe her and read how ineradicable was her love for Laxmi, how inconsolable her grief.

She rides the slide away from the chemical reek of frozen flesh that lingers over the 'mart, and heads towards the sub-orb station beneath the effigy of Christ. At this time of day the scream that haunts the world is not so pronounced. It's at the beginning of its cycle, a subliminal howl that Sabine can tolerate. Later, the scream will increase and play havoc with telepathic awareness around the world. And for Sabine it will be especially painful.

She takes her seat aboard the sub-orb shuttle, just another Europebound cosmopolite. Her face is a mix of Oriental and Scandinavian: skin the colour of mocha, severe slant eyes and golden dreadlocks swept back in a fiery comet's tail.

Five hours later she's in Lisbon and the brainscream, a keening crescendo of almost physical agony, makes the thought of oblivion an attractive option.

Sabine Savatageot met Laxmi Patel in the capital of the United States of India.

Five years ago Sabine took a holiday in Benares. The city was everything she had expected it to be – dirty, noisy and overcrowded. To escape the chaos she spent many a warm evening wandering through the narrow alleys on the banks of the Ganges. After watching the cremations on the ghats she'd return slowly to her hotel, the scent of woodsmoke and cooking flesh leaving a bitter taste in her mouth.

She found Laxmi between a rickety stack of cola crates and the micro-laser stand of a gem-cutter. She'd been reading occasionally on the way back from the river, browsing in the alien territory of the Hindu mind. And she'd been aware of Laxmi's emanations long before she actually saw the girl. At first she assumed that the discordant mindmush was the product of some pained animal, a rabid dog or crippled temple monkey. Then she turned a corner and the truth blitzed her.

Until then Sabine had dismissed claims of 'love at first sight' as the retroactive illusion of incurable romantics – something that she, who could always read the truth behind superficial beauty, had never been prey to. Nevertheless she experienced it now, chaotically and irrationally – for Laxmi was a limbless torso slung recumbent on the woven twine of a hand-made charpoy.

The stump of her naked body was patched with pressure sores and cross-hatched with bloody weals in the pattern of the lattice.

Sabine stared at the girl and failed to see the diseased, kohl-rimmed eyes that gazed out blindly, or the greasy lice-infested hair. She probed deeper, and found the girl's mind to be as crippled and malformed as her body. Sabine saw only the beauty of her martyred face, though – and that which she might become.

The gem-cutter, squatting over his work, noticed her appalled fascination and proffered a palm for baksheesh. Sabine fled.

The following day she made enquiries.

Laxmi was fourteen, and an orphan. Her parents had perished in the monsoon floods of '57 and she had been taken in by her uncle, the gem-cutter, and his wife. Born without limbs, she was blind, meningital and brain-damaged. And Harijan too, as if her physical afflictions were not enough. Sabine hired a medic who told her that the girl would be dead within six months – which would be fine by the gem-cutter. As far as he was concerned, Laxmi had earned her present terrible condition through ill-deeds committed in a previous life. Death would be a release, an opportunity perhaps to improve her karmic standing.

And Sabine might have agreed that death would be a merciful release, had she not been aware of the wonders of medical technology.

One week after finding Laxmi, Sabine bought her for ten thousand creds.

She had the girl dispatched to Rio and installed in an expensive total resurrection clinic. To pay for Laxmi's rebirth she probed minds overtime. She chose to stay away from Rio, retaining the mental picture of Laxmi on the charpoy to one day match against the miraculous fact of the resurrected woman. The medics supplied her with progress reports from month to month. They chose to work first on the girl's physical disabilities, and flushed from her system the meningital virus and others lurking there. They straightened her spine, adding vertebrae, and remodelled her deformed pelvic flanges to accommodate the vat-nurtured hips and legs grafted on six months into the operation. They gave her slim arms and big brown eyes, and then began work on her mind. They boosted her IQ with synthetic cortical implants and a small occipital computer, with input sockets jacked direct to the learning centres of her brain to facilitate the crash-course of lessons programmed over the next year. The medics suggested a childhood-analogue implant, but on Sabine's instructions she was told the truth of her origins. At the time, the thought of Laxmi living a lie with no knowledge of the truth filled Sabine with horror. Only later did she wonder how much this was because she wanted the girl to know that it was she who had saved her life.

Two years after the first operation, Laxmi walked from the clinic. She had Sabine's tag and stack location, but instead of getting in touch she returned to India. After a year's training she joined the United Indian spacefleet. Her first bigship was the *Pride of Udaipur*, an exploration vessel bound for the Crab Nebula, six thousand light years from Earth.

Laxmi was seventeen. And the first Harijan in space.

Sabine has an hour to kill before her rendezvous with Østergaart. She chooses an outdoor cafe on the paved *Praça do Comercio*, sips brandy and fixes her attention on the wide, blue River Tagus. She orders a second drink, then a third. This has nothing to do with her apprehension at the meeting with Ø, dread it though she does.

The brainhowl is more of a screech now, a cerebral assault of white noise. Sabine can barely take the pain, but the drinks help. She is sweating, and her hand shakes as she lifts the glass. From time to time she finds herself trying to single out the chord of

Laxmi's agony from the whole, but she knows that this is impossible. The existential scream emanates from the eleven Indian crew members as well as from Laxmi – a concerted cry of torture beyond individual identification.

As always, as if to illustrate Sabine's painful isolation, the people around her are happily unaware: tourists stroll casually; a party of schoolchildren runs through the streets; the waiter serves her and smiles without a care. Everything is normal, running smooth. Only grade-one telepaths are cursed with the interstellar cry.

Towards the end of the hour, as she gets up and leaves the cafe, the pain begins to diminish. She is aware of a certain diminuendo as the daily emission reaches the low-point of its cycle. She strolls across the square and into the quartz dodecahedron of the Historical Participatorium.

Oddly, for a weekday, it is closed. However, a slim young man attracts her attention in the foyer and escorts her into a downchute. They pass through a pair of swing doors into the darkened auditorium. Sabine takes a few steps forward, then looks round to find the boy gone. She walks through the darkness between rows of seats. "Østergaart?"

And instantly a vertical column of light illuminates the circular stage in the well of the amphitheatre. On the stage, arranged in the frozen postures they arrived at when the last performance closed, are a dozen figures in orange robes, seated around Buddha in the lotus position beneath a Bo tree.

Østergaart, immaculate in a jet black one-piece suit, makes his entrance from stage left. He is tall and tanned and impossibly handsome, and the fact that he has changed not at all in five years is testimony to the artificiality of his appearance.

Sabine finds this another excuse to dislike the man. Although she makes use of all the latest medical advances, as an aid to her profession, she has done nothing to remove the lines and wrinkles that age and experience have etched on her face. Østergaart's perfection is the symptom of a vanity that Sabine considers tantamount to a character defect.

She is glad she is shielded now, so that Ø cannot read her thoughts. Then again, if he could probe her he might realise how much she dislikes him, leave her alone for good.

Østergaart assumes a foursquare pose centre-stage and smiles down at her. "It's been a long time, Sabine. When did we last meet?" He feigns intense recollection. "Paris, last Summer? You recall, we dined at the Eiffel gastrodome."

She stares at him, defiant. "What do you want?"

Ø's look suddenly hardens. "Not what you think, Miss Savatageot. This is purely business. Please, sit down." He indicates a seat in the front row of the auditorium.

Sabine obeys, her relief tempered by suspicion at why he needs to see her in person. She does not trust Ø. A man with his power does not so easily cease the chase.

"The reason I called you here..." Ø says. "I regard you as the finest telepath I have, Sabine."

She remains silent, staring at him.

"You deserve promotion."

As Sabine is already grade-one, and in the highest pay bracket for teleheads, she wonders just what 'promotion' might mean. "Partnership in the company?" she suggests, sarcastic.

"I mean a promotion of ability, of telepower. I want to make your ability more powerful than it is already..." And lets it hang.

It takes seconds for Sabine to see the implications. "*More* powerful?" she laughs. "Listen, I can hardly take the scream now. Just how the hell do you think I'd survive with it *amplified*?" And she trembles with rage as if, by what he's suggesting, Østergaart is somehow trying to devalue the pain of her loss.

"Let me explain, Sabine. You'd undergo an operation to fit an occipital computer and an implant in your cerebellum. You would have the ability, then, to deal with genetics."

"Racial memories?"

"Not quite," Ø says. "Please put on the headphones."

Each seat is equipped with a pair of 'phones, and Sabine clamps the padded ear-muffs around her head. Østergaart leaves the stage and seconds later the scene comes to life. The robot beneath the tree begins to move and speak – and it's as if Sabine is inside Siddhartha Gautama's cranium, participating in this historical recreation. With a little concentration she can almost forget that she is herself. The effect is similar to that of total immersion in the psyche of one of her subjects, with the difference that whereas her subjects are invariably bad, Buddha is *good.*

She wonders how this effect is achieved.

"Okay," Østergaart says. On stage the robot winds down, is left frozen midway through a beatific gesture. Sabine feels a swift sense of regret as the good brainvibes subside. Ø emerges from the wings and gestures for her to come up on stage.

They cross to the seated robot that plays the part of Buddha. Østergaart reaches out and folds back the ear. "Look," he says. And Sabine sees the legend ØSTERGAART INDUSTRIES printed small around the inside.

"All this belongs to you?"

"I initiated the Historical Participatoriums a year ago."

"How does this fit in with genetics?"

"Years ago, before I started the Agency, I was involved in experimental psionic research at the Oslo Institute. I had a gene-telepath probe the area of the brain so far unused, that vast untapped reservoir of potential, and found the stacked genetic material of ancestors going back to the very start of time. Last year I located the descendants of famous people, from Jesus to

Hitler, Buddha to Genghis Khan. For limited periods my telepath could bring forth certain individuals to inhabit present-day bodies. She could not maintain the connection indefinitely, but for just long enough to record thought-process analogues, which is what you experienced just now. We have done it with a few hundred subjects so far, some more successfully than others."

"If your genetic telepath can do this," Sabine says, "I don't see why you need me."

"Natalia was killed in the Helsinki sub-orb disaster last month," Ø replies. "You are her replacement. My surgeons will fit you with a small implant, and after the operation you will be able to summon ancestors to inhabit the bodies of their descendants on... shall we say, a 'time-share' basis."

Sabine does not say so, but to her this facility seems more like a demotion: from apprehending criminals to recreating historical personalities for the entertainment industry.

She gestures to the stage and the static players. "I presume the ability will be used to greater effect than just...?"

Ø smiles to himself. "Look," he says, and indicates the backcloth. As Sabine watches, a hologram appears. The portrait is that of a Chinese bigship captain, upstanding and proud in the uniform of the Peoples' Spacefleet.

"Xian Cheng," Ø says. "The former captain of the *Lao Tzu*. He and his crew were the first Earthmen to explore the Nilakantha Stardrift, and specifically the Earthlike planet of star Kalki."

Sabine feels suddenly faint. "I don't see..."

"Cheng was in command of a landing party that explored Kalki II. He was the only member of that party to make it back to the ship – six others perished in mysterious circumstances. Cheng never fully recovered from the ordeal; whatever fate befell the scientists also, to a lesser degree, affected him. He could not explain what had happened on the planet, and this was before the time of telepaths. He was discharged from the service and the Nilakantha Stardrift was declared off-limits. Until a year ago, that is."

Sabine nods, wordless. Østergaart continues, "Cheng went into retreat and entered a Buddhist monastery in the state of Tibet. He died a few years later without ever fully recounting what happened on that landfall. Then, one month ago, I learned that on his return from the 'drift he had fathered a daughter."

Sabine begins to see a pattern to the events of the past hour. Before she can speak, Ø goes on, "The scream is wreaking havoc with all grade-ones, Sabine. The underworld doesn't know exactly what's happening, but they're suddenly finding their crimes going unsolved. This cannot continue. I need an answer." He stares directly at Sabine, waiting.

She whispers, "His daughter...?"

He nods. "You will probe his daughter, access Captain Xian Cheng and bring him forth. We will then be able to find out what happened on Kalki II, perhaps even learn enough to help us combat the scream." Østergaart smiles. "And there will be one added bonus, for you."

She looks at him. "And that will be?"

"You will be able to control your tele-ability by the simple expedient of switching off the occipital computer. For you, then, the scream will no longer exist."

The thought that at last she might find out what terrible fate befell her lover fills her with a mixture of relief and dread. She tries to imagine what it will be like to control the only thing that connects her to Laxmi – and some sense of martyrdom makes her wonder if she might from time to time access the scream, to experience again the delicious pain of self-pity.

Then her suspicion of Østergaart returns. Does he have an ulterior motive for offering her this release? Does he think that her love for Laxmi might be diminished when she is no longer torn by the primal scream?

At that second, the scream makes itself known again in the back of her mind; it begins its return on an upward cycle.

"When can I have the operation?" Sabine asks.

"How about tonight? I have my surgeons ready and waiting in Montreal."

Sabine inclines her head in assent. She tells herself that only when she finds out what happened, all those light years away on Kalki II, will she be able to help Laxmi.

Sabine and Ø leave the auditorium together.

Sabine was living in Switzerland a year back when Laxmi returned from her first tour of duty to the Out-there. Between shifts she partied with film stars and Euro-politicians and tried to forget that the *Pride of Udaipur* was docked in Mumbai. Often she'd try to analyse her motives in saving the Indian girl, and had to admit that it was in part prompted by some deep, maternal instinct. In Sabine's idealised scenario of the future, Laxmi would fill the role of lover and daughter, and as the time passed and Laxmi failed to contact her, it hurt Sabine that she was neither.

Then one morning, as she breakfasted on the patio overlooking Lake Geneva, she had a visitor. She saw the small figure climbing the switch-back steps that serviced the apartment, but assumed it was the owner of a residence higher up the hill. Only as the woman approached the patio, and Sabine saw that she was Asian, did the realisation hit her.

She paused by the rail, shielding her eyes from the sun and smiling at Sabine. Her radiation silvers were cut off above knee and elbow, and on the swell of her chest was the multi-armed Shiva logo of the United Indian Spacefleet.

Sabine thought back to the pitiful torso of four years ago, and it was hard to credit that this pretty eighteen-year-old was the same person. "Laxmi... it *is* you, isn't it?"

The woman's smile widened, glacial enamel against brown skin. Her eyes were alight. Sabine stood, tipping her chair, and they embraced. Then she pulled away and laughed, tearful. "This is ridiculous! I hardly know you..." She probed, experienced the woman's warmth, her affection, and then out of propriety withdrew and allowed Laxmi to speak.

They spent the following six months together. Laxmi had furlough due, and Sabine was granted long-service leave from the Østergaart Agency. They rented a villa at the coastal resort of Manakara, Madagascar, and divided their time between exploring each other and the island.

Sabine loved the spacer for what she had become, a gifted and genuine person in her own right, above and beyond the intellectual advantage bestowed by the cortical implants: technology could grant intellect, but only experience and reflection brought wisdom. Often Sabine would read the Indian woman, and in Laxmi's mind she saw herself as the mother Laxmi had never known, a focus of maternal permanence in a chaotic continuum, a companion, friend and lover.

Then, towards the end of the six months, a summons arrived for Laxmi from the United Indian Spacefleet.

They spent the last night together on the balcony of their villa and watched the sun sink into the Indian ocean. "Where?" Sabine asked, indicating the massed stars.

"I'm supposed to tell no-one," Laxmi whispered, and pointed. "See that veil? There. The Nilakantha Stardrift."

Sabine drew away from the Indian to look at her. The name was familiar. "Isn't that...?"

Laxmi nodded. "It was off-limits until just recently. We're going in there to take another look."

"You take care, okay?" She kissed Laxmi and tried to forget that she was leaving in the morning.

Six months later Sabine caught a newscast which reported that the crew of the *Pride of Udaipur* had perished in the 'drift. A later report corrected this. The crew had suffered serious injuries on the planet of Kalki II, and the Android back-up team had rescued them and was piloting the bigship back to Earth.

And around that time the scream began.

Twelve hours after the operation Sabine takes the sub-orb from Montreal and rendezvous with Østergaart in Rome. She is aware of a slight discomfort at the base of her skull, where the teflon bulge of the occipital computer obtrudes through her skin, and from time to time she suffers acute, stabbing migraines. But this is a small price to pay for the banishment of the scream. For the first time in months she can relax without the constant, piercing presence of the nightmare in her head.

At Rome, the cortical implant bleeds instructions into her consciousness. She locates Østergaart in the arrivals lounge and he leads her from the terminal to a waiting ground-effect vehicle. A chauffeur steers them from the parking stack and into the hills.

Østergaart remains silent for a while, then glances across at her. "The implant becomes you," he murmurs, referring to the ring of black metal that encircles her neck like a choker.

Sabine ignores him, leans back and stares into the night sky. She finds the blue-shifted haze of the Nilakantha Stardrift, a shimmering veil a degree above the horizon. Somewhere out there, she knows, the *Pride of Udaipur* is lighting back through the void to Earth. Without the cerebral verification of the scream she finds it almost impossible to believe.

Østergaart clears his throat, then says casually, "While you were under... there was a report from the Androids piloting the *Udaipur*."

Sabine stares at him, suddenly aware of her heartbeat.

"The first officer died on Kalki II. The rest of the crew are in suspension now."

"But the scream...?" Sabine is almost pleading. "What happened to them?" Though when she says 'them' she is thinking only of Laxmi.

Ø looks away. He seems reluctant to divulge this information. "According to reports received, the landing party was attacked by the natives of the planet. Only the intervention of the Andys saved further casualties."

"Attacked...?" Sabine is incredulous.

"Perhaps we'll find out more when you probe Xian Cheng."

In less than an hour they arrive at their destination.

The hotel is a towering needle supported by three scimitar-shaped legs. Between the flaring stand, and beneath the obelisk of the hotel itself, a vast glass bauble slowly rotates. Inside, a party is in progress. The sight of air-taxis landing, and affluent guests stepping out, triggers an information release in Sabine's implant. The party is in celebration of the successful Procyon probe, and the guests are the crew of the *Leonardo da Vinci* and executives from the Fellini Organisation. Østergaart has managed to obtain tickets, and they pass inside.

Sabine and Ø separate and circulate. This is the first time since the operation that Sabine is aware she is no longer telepathic. Her ability is switched off, and the party seems dead to her. Usually, she would be picking up a thousand different emotions from the party-goers, and responding to them on an individual basis. However, when she finds herself among a group of Italian spacers recalling the spiraldown to the surface of Procyon IV, she learns that she has been programmed with all the technical information about the probe. She joins in like one of the team. And in Italian, too.

Thanks to her occipital, she resembles a spacer: most of the guests are computer-assisted, and sport a variety of implants from small occipital gadgets like Sabine's, to larger, cumbersome extra-cranial units for achieving interface-integration with shipboard matrices.

Across the room, on the dance floor, Sabine sees Østergaart dancing with a young Chinese woman in the uniform of the Italian Spacefleet: Xian Cheng's daughter, Lin.

Later, as instructed, Sabine leaves the party and takes the upchute to a suite on the top floor. The door opens to her palm print. She locates the bedroom and steps out onto the balcony, drawing the shimmer-stream curtain behind her. She reclines on the lounger, stares into the night sky and locates again the scintillating beauty of the Nilakantha Stardrift.

As she awaits the arrival of Ø and Lin Cheng, she considers what little is known about the first Terran expedition to the 'drift. Since Captain Xian Cheng was the sole survivor from the landing party, and he was in no condition to submit a coherent report, the only record of what happened on Kalki II was that of the ship's first officer.

Kalki II is the dying world of a dying sun, a jungle-and-ocean planet inhabited by a species of small humanoid aliens. They are arboreal creatures, similar to the Terran ape, and inhabit the jungles of the planet's largest continent. This much was discovered by unmanned probes two years before the arrival of the *Lao Tzu*.

Three days after touchdown, Cheng took a landing party into the jungle. They set up camp and attempted to establish contact with the aliens. The following day Cheng returned to the ship to file a report to Earth. There was no hint in his dispatch of the tragedy about to befall the exploration party. Everything was running smoothly – a model planetfall, he called it.

On Cheng's return to the campsite, he contacted his first officer aboard the ship and reported that the rest of his team were missing. He intended searching the surrounding jungle for them, and requested assistance. One hour later the first officer and an engineer found Cheng in the jungle in a state approaching terror; they found also the bodies of the exploration party. Autopsies performed on-ship revealed that they had died of heart failure consistent with having undergone extreme shock. The *Lao Tzu* lighted from Kalki II the following day.

All this happened before the age of surgically-induced telepathy; there was no way of learning from Cheng what had occurred to him between the time of his last radio report and when the first officer found him. Whatever killed his men had inflicted the captain with amnesia, and the events of the landfall remained a mystery.

Sabine stares at the lights of the city spread out below. She is tortured by the memory of the scream, now no more than an elusive echo in her head. The events of that first mission have repeated themselves to a lesser – though in a way more horrific – extent thirty years later. Laxmi and eleven of her crewmates have survived, though exactly what they have survived is a secret known only to themselves and Captain Xian Cheng.

Sabine regards the task ahead of her with ambivalence.

She hears a noise from within the bedroom. Ø calls her name and Sabine steps from the balcony. The small Chinese girl is arranging herself demurely on the bed, smiling up at Østergaart. Sabine wonders how much Ø paid the girl to undergo the process.

As the High Priestess of this unique ceremony, Sabine kneels beside the circular bed and, as instructed by another information-release from her implant, takes Lin Cheng's brow between her fingers. Sabine hesitates, and then speaks the command, a techno-mantra that activates the mechanism buried within her head. She dives into the ocean of Lin Cheng's consciousness, and the computer takes over and utilises Sabine's ability to its own ends. For her convenience, the programme fits her into a structured-reality analogue: she is aware that what she is experiencing is just the symbolic representation of what is in fact a techno-chemical process. She finds herself on the lower 'rung' of a spiral ladder that extends above her into infinity. As she moves up and around the helix she is conscious of human forms, suspended in placenta-like sacs to her right and left: on one side she senses masculinity, on the other femininity. Sabine is drawn to the right, towards the essence of someone she recognises as Captain Xian Cheng. She enters his sphere and draws him out, as instructed. She slides with him down around the helter-skelter of the helix and then, with a jolt that tells her she has arrived, she finds herself once again in the room and kneeling by the bed. She is covered in sweat and shaking from the exertion of bringing Xian Cheng into being. Østergaart, she realises with shock, is holding her. She pulls herself away.

She glances at the figure on the bed. Lin Cheng lies unconscious, her face serene.

Østergaart touches a control on his neck and closes his eyes, probing for Xian Cheng's secret.

Not to be left out, Sabine instructs her implant to activate her tele-ability and dives through the scream and into Xian Cheng's chaotic psyche. She is buffeted by his psychosis like a leaf in a hurricane, and his recollection of the planetfall is not difficult to find. It haunts his subconscious like a screaming banshee, and Sabine has no trouble easing herself into his memory of the early stages of the expedition.

She is with him as he returns to the ship and makes his report to Earth, then sets out again with a carrycase of supplies. He reaches the clearing and finds the first tent-dome empty. He drops the 'case and runs to the next dome, unease rising within him as he finds that this too has been vacated. At the far end of the clearing, where a path leads further into the jungle, he notices the signs of a disturbance; soil has been kicked up, undergrowth broken. He guesses that the team made a sighting of an alien and rushed out to follow it. He calls his first officer back at the ship and requests assistance, then sets off at a run into the jungle.

He arrives at the next clearing and halts, for what he sees through the twilight of the undergrowth fills him with fear. The six scientists are sprawled about the clearing, unconscious, though it is not their disablement that horrifies him.

Squatting on the chest of each scientist is a small creature the size of an ape, but hairless; something about their proprietorial postures suggests malevolence. Each creature has one hand over a scientist's face, long fingers spanning their foreheads.

Cheng utters a low moan at the sight of this and backs from the clearing, but before he can turn and run an alien leaps at him, hitting his chest and forcing him to the ground. It clings to him and reaches out for his face... and Cheng is powerless to resist.

What happens next, Sabine realises distantly, is what killed Cheng's scientists, and what would have killed Laxmi and her colleagues but for their rescue by the Androids.

The alien touches Cheng, and in that first second of contact Sabine is aware that it means no harm. It does not intend to kill or even frighten the Earthman. This, among the natives of Kalki II, is a ritual form of greeting – a sharing of one individual's consciousness with another. Unfortunately for the Terrans, the aliens possess so unique and disturbing a view of reality that the human mind finds such knowledge impossible to assimilate, and then simply terrifying.

The aliens are aware of the process of entropy not just as an abstract concept as humans understand it, but as a physical and observable phenomenon. When the alien communicates with

Cheng, he – and, through him, Sabine – has a shattering glimpse of the dissolution of the universe. They witness decay on a cosmic scale: the coming apart of the atom, which in reality covers immeasurable aeons, is compressed into a time-span they can comprehend. Reality is revealed in a condition of constant annihilation. Cheng is about to scream, and Sabine with him, when the alien breaks contact and scurries away.

The natives are gathered at the far side of the clearing, staring mutely at the scientists as if in disbelief at their deaths. Then, suddenly, they scatter into the jungle and disappear. Cheng manages to gather himself and stagger back towards the ship, and an hour later he is found – ranting and delirious – by the first officer and an engineer.

Sabine finds herself reliving the point of contact with the appalling alien vision. She dives into the sensation again and again. Cheng escaped full contact and survived; his scientists were over-exposed, and perished as a result. Laxmi and her colleagues, it is now clear, experienced contact between these degrees, and screamed with a psychic agony that ripped through the void and communicated with receptive minds on Earth. At last Sabine comes to understand their pain.

And she screams.

Three days later Sabine has recovered sufficiently to travel. She takes the sub-orb to Mumbai and meets Østergaart at the spaceport.

He restrains Sabine with a gentle hand on her arm.

She regards him.

Ø is uneasy. "Please... have you considered this? Laxmi is in pain... She's no longer the person you knew. It would be easier for you if..."

"If I just walked away and tried to forget about it?"

"I didn't mean it like that."

After security clearance, they are driven across the wide-open, dusty apron of the arrivals' field. In the distance, *The Pride of Udaipur* squats on its hydraulics like some malevolent, alien reptile. Yet to undergo a repaint job after its journey through the void, the Udaipur presents an excoriated and battle-scarred exterior. At the sight of it, and all it represents, Sabine experiences the sickness of grief rising within her.

She considers activating her tele-ability so that she might have some contact with Laxmi, however terrible that contact might be. She decides against it; she is not that much of a martyr.

The Pride of Udaipur has been dirtside two days now and, according to Østergaart, the proximity of the source of the scream has scoured the heads of *every* telepath on Earth, not just grade-ones as before. Many have been driven insane and, in Ø's Agency alone, three to suicide.

Sabine asks, "Can anything be done?"

Østergaart indicates a fleet of trucks positioning themselves around the bigship. Massive baffles, like radio-telescopes, are being erected alongside the *Udaipur's* flanks. "I have my finest engineers working on some way of muffling the scream."

"I meant," Sabine says, "for Laxmi and the crew."

"Oh." Østergaart is silent for a second, chastened. "There's a team of medics working on them as we speak."

They make the rest of the journey in comparative quiet. From time to time, Ø speaks into his handset, liaising with his engineers. They drive into the hold of the bigship via a ramp and climb from the shuttle. A uniformed official leads them to the suspension chamber.

They arrive at a triangular door, point down, which lifts to reveal a similarly shaped chamber. The floor is a narrow strip down which they walk. On either sloping side are set half a dozen suspension pods. Around each one is a team of medics.

Ø steers Sabine to the pod containing the Indian Spacer she had once known as Laxmi Patel, and she steels herself for the shock.

Laxmi is no longer young and attractive. The experience she has undergone on Kalki II has aged her, turned her hair grey and scored deep, unnatural lines in her face. The old woman is arched, as if in a prolonged spasm of pain.

At the evidence of Laxmi's physical agony, Sabine wants to activate her tele-ability so that she might join her lover in her suffering. But something stops her, something more than just the fear of pain.

Laxmi's rolling eyes locate Sabine and lock on. The contact sends a jolt through Sabine, paralysing her. She is aware of Ø and the medics, watching.

Laxmi reaches out, not to take Sabine's hand in a gesture of greeting, but to point in accusation.

The sinews of her neck stand out, and her lips form a rictus as if to scream. But all that comes out is a grating whisper. "*Why...?*"

"Laxmi?" Sabine cries.

Then, "You should have... let me die!"

As she stares down at the tortured woman, she thinks back to the afternoon five years ago when she first discovered Laxmi on the charpoy, and the irony of the situation slices through her and twists like a blade.

She turns to Østergaart.

He stands in consultation with his medics, and then slowly shakes his head.

"I'm sorry..."

Sabine runs from the chamber, conscious only of the need for air. She stands at the top of the ramp, breathing deeply and staring out over the spaceport.

Down below, the first of the trucks drives away, taking a baffle with it, and only then does she begin to weep.

She is aware of Ø at her side.

"I know how you feel," he says.

She stares at him. "Do you?"

"I saved *you* once, Sabine."

He looks at her with an expression in his eyes that might be compassion, and then takes her hand in his.

THE THALLIAN INTERVENTION

24th May, 1926.

I cannot bring myself to go onto the deck and stare into the night sky. I know very well that I should, if I wish to learn the truth; but in all honesty I am too frightened to leave my cabin... Perhaps later, when I've managed to calm my nerves and order my thoughts. First I will set down the events of the voyage so far, try to make some sense of the situation. Then and only then will I leave the cabin and stare into the night sky, and learn the terrible truth.

Three days ago I boarded the liner at Singapore, bound for Southampton. I made the acquaintance of Benjamin J. Cadwallader at breakfast in the dining room on the first full day of the voyage. A tall man of middle years, he entered the room and took the table next to mine. He held himself in a stiff manner that suggested illness, and carried under his arm, as a pastor might carry a book of psalms, a familiar volume on the strategy of chess.

I introduced myself, mentioning that clearly he too was a student of the Game. His grey eyes fixed me with a penetrating gaze, studying me in minute detail. Then he shook my hand awkwardly, as if he were unaccustomed to the gesture.

"Indeed I am," he replied, in an accent I could not place. "Do you play?"

"I most certainly do."

His face was thin, though his brow was broad, and the eyes beneath of a grey and far away aspect I am only now coming to understand.

Mr Cadwallader informed me that he had owned a rubber plantation in Malayasia, until his retirement one month ago. I did not enquire, but I suspected, from his frail appearance, that ill health might have forced his premature return to the West.

We finished breakfast and went our separate ways.

I saw nothing of Mr Cadwallader for three days, and when I did meet him again he seemed in an even feebler state of health.

I was taking lunch in the dining room when he entered and seated himself at my table with a smile and a few words of greeting. When we had finished our respective meals, his distant eyes met mine. For a second, they took on what I can only describe as a look of speculation.

"I wonder, Mr Meredith, if you would do me the honour of consenting to a game or two of chess?"

"The pleasure would be mine," I said.

"If we could stage the contest in my cabin, I would be grateful. My health, as you might have noticed, is not the best. I have certain medicaments which I must take at regular intervals."

"By all means," I said, and after coffee we walked to his room.

He fumbled with the key in the door, then turned to me on the threshold. "If you will be so kind as to wait outside for just one moment..." he said, and without explanation closed the door before me. I heard the key turn in the lock. Then, as if this were not odd enough, I heard from within the cabin the sound of something of great weight being dragged across the floor. A minute later the door opened and Mr Cadwallader appeared, his exertions showing in a sheen of sweat that covered his haggard features.

His cabin was identical to my own. The connecting door to the bed-chamber, I noticed, was closed. Two bulky armchairs faced each other across a small table. Cadwallader invited me to take a seat.

We arranged our pieces and settled down to do battle. Mr Cadwallader won the first game, and I the second. By the third, his manner seemed abstracted; it was as if he were awaiting a call or summons. Even so, he beat me, then sank back into his chair with a look of exhaustion. "Forgive me, but the effort... I must rest. Perhaps we might play again tomorrow?"

"I understand perfectly," I said. "Perhaps in the afternoon?"

"I am afraid I will be indisposed at that time. But if you would be so kind as to drop by tomorrow evening..."

I accepted his invitation, and was opening the door when a curious, shrill double-note issued from the direction of his bedroom. I turned, and was in time to see Mr Cadwallader hoist himself from his chair and limp to the bedroom door, which he closed firmly behind him.

I spent a good part of the following day in my cabin, and at eight that evening left to keep my appointment with Mr Cadwallader.

I knocked on the door, and then again. I waited a minute, and still there was no reply. It occurred to me that perhaps my friend's health had taken a turn for the worse. I tried the handle, then pushed open the door and stepped inside. I found Mr Cadwallader seated in his armchair, apparently asleep. I took one step forward – and revised my opinion. Cadwallader seemed dead, such was his immobility.

I was about to leave and summon the ship's doctor when Mr Cadwallader suddenly opened his eyes. A smile of recognition warmed his features. He seemed to come to life by degrees, like an automaton.

I mumbled something about finding his door unlocked, but Cadwallader waved aside my explanation.

"Meredith," he said. "Please be seated. Would you care for a drop of brandy?" He indicated a decanter beside the chessboard.

I set up the pieces and he poured two good measures. I proposed a toast, wishing him well on his visit to the old country.

We began a game, which Mr Cadwallader won within twenty moves, and as I admitted defeat he refilled our glasses.

He showed no inclination to begin another game. He smiled at me over the board. "You are a man of liberal views," he said. "Would I be correct in thinking that I could trust you?"

I nodded. "You would," I said.

He began to ask many questions, and while I answered them he seemed to pay little regard to the actual answers. His grey eyes stared at me – *through* me; seeing me but at the same time, I felt, inspecting my soul.

"Yes," he said. "Yes, as I suspected..."

"You suspected what?" I asked.

"From the beginning," Cadwallader said, "I knew you were the man I was seeking."

"Seeking?" I repeated.

"Mr Meredith," he said, regarding me intensely, "would it surprise you to learn that that this planet is not alone in harbouring intelligent life?"

I lowered my glass, quite shocked. I managed, "To be perfectly honest I cannot recall ever giving the matter much consideration."

"I am under strict instructions from my Commanding Officer not to breathe a word of my mission to any native of this planet. My present circumstances, however, force me to disobey that order."

I stared at him. "Your Commanding Officer? Your... *mission?*"

"I am from the planet Thallia, of the star known to you as Bellatrix, and I am here in my capacity as an engineer–"

"An engineer?"

"An engineer of Temporal Alignment."

I shook my head. "Temporal Alignment...? I'm afraid I..." My head was spinning, and the brandy was not accountable.

His thin smile hyphenated his sallow cheeks, and I was aware that, for the moment, his illness seemed to recede.

"Perhaps I had better begin at the beginning."

"Perhaps you had," I agreed.

He regarded me above his joined finger-tips. "In three thousand years," he began, "my planet will be the only one boasting intelligent life in the entire galaxy."

"But what about Earth? Surely in three thousand years..."

He smiled sadly. "I will come to that presently," he informed me. "As I said, we Thallians will then be the only intelligent race in the galaxy. The chances of two sentient races existing at the same time in the same galaxy are astronomical – billions to one. My race, at the peak of its technological development, finds itself alone. Can you conceive of that, Mr Meredith? No, I rather think you cannot. We have developed sciences that would seem to you like magic; yet we have no one with whom to share this great store of knowledge. We have the means to help planets, civilisations, through potentially catastrophic periods of their history – yet no planetary civilisations co-existed with our own."

He paused, his eyes glazed as if contemplating some far distant future time. Presently he continued, "Throughout the galaxy we sent survey ships, searching for intelligent life. Alas, they found only the remains of life, races devolved into barbarism, civilisations that had destroyed themselves through avaricious power struggles. Then, our scientists made a remarkable breakthrough: they discovered the secret of time travel. More, they also learnt how to bring into alignment with our own time those planets which we had found in ruination – *but at a period of those planets' histories when they were bursting with life and intelligence!*"

He sipped his brandy, giving me time to digest this information. "But," I said, humouring him, "how is it that you can 'align' these civilisations which your survey ships locate in ruins? There is a paradox here, if I rightly understand the matter. Surely the very fact that your ships locate a planet in ruination suggests that you do not 'align' that planet?"

"That is astute of you," he said. "There is certainly a paradox, though this is easily explained."

He sat back, clasped his hands before his chest, and continued. "It is the duty of a Temporal Engineer to set up a rift in the space-time continuum around the subject planet. This has the effect of opening two separate time-streams, so that, literally, time will fork. There will be a planet which will find itself in the 'future', co-existent with Thallia, and we will then help the planet through its time of crisis; and there will be a planet which continues on its downward path to ruination and extinction."

"But how is this... this *space-time rift* brought about?" I asked impatiently.

"First," Cadwallader replied, "the planet's nodal point must be located; this is the only locus on the subject planet at which the rift can be effected – the planet's chronic weak spot, if you like."

"And then?"

"And then the apparatus known as the Temporal Equalizer comes into play."

"The device you have set up in your bedroom?" I ventured, the full implications of Cadwallader's mission becoming apparent to me. "You..." I said, "you intend to *align* Earth?"

"As a Temporal Engineer it is my duty to bring Earth 'up to date' as we joke."

"But... but this suggests that in time the Earth will be no more!"

He inclined his head. "In one time-stream, this is so."

"But how can humankind possibly bring ruination upon the Earth? This is preposterous!"

Again that thin, wintery smile occurred on his haggard face. "In a little over one hundred and fifty years, Mr Meredith, humankind will have destroyed itself – in one time-line it has already happened, through conflicts utilising germ warfare and chemical poisons. These evils will eradicate not only humankind from the face of the Earth, but every other form of life as well. We wish to align the Earth and guide you through this time of crisis, for humankind has the potential for genius as well as a penchant for self-destruction." His smile was benign.

I shook my head. "I find this hard to believe."

"Perhaps if you were present at the time of the alignment..."

I looked up. "This will be performed in England?"

"I have every reason to believe that the Earth's nodal point is situated in the Indian ocean."

"And you will effect the rift in transit?"

"As to whether I will effect the rift..." He smiled at me. "I began this exchange by placing my trust in you. I have told you a tale that could, if you cared to broadcast it, have me certified as a lunatic – certainly I have courted your incredulity. I have not, I must add, told you this tale for the good of my health–" and here he gave a snort of laughter. "In short, I need your help – indeed your planet needs your help. I have a very short time left in which to live; I have contracted some Earthly virus that is rapidly killing me. In all probability I will be dead in little over a day."

He stared at me, his face expressionless.

"What can I do–?" I began.

A sound like a sigh of relief escaped his perished lips. "For the time being, nothing. But, if you would be so kind as to meet me in this cabin at five o'clock tomorrow evening, I will acquaint you with your duty. Until then..." Unable to rise from his armchair, he lifted his hand in dismissal.

I passed a sleepless night, my head full of Mr Cadwallader's fantastic tale. I awoke early and spent the remainder of the day pacing the deck.

It came to me that the mysterious Mr Cadwallader was nothing more than a scribbler of the genre known as 'Scientific Romance'. He had got into his head the fantastic plot for his next story, and had tried it out on me. That was it! No doubt, when five o'clock arrived, Mr Cadwallader would be all smiles and apologies as he explained to me his magnificent practical joke.

After a bite of afternoon tea, I took myself to his cabin and rapped upon the door. Again I received no reply; again, I took it upon myself to open the door.

"Cadwallader," I called heartily as I crossed the threshold. "Your game is up!"

My voice dried in my throat and I stopped dead as, from beyond the open door of the bedroom, I saw an eerie white light. It pulsed in a regular rhythm and fitfully illuminated the gloom of the cabin. It was by this light that I made out Mr Cadwallader.

He was sprawled upon a *chaise longue* at the far end of the room, and on seeing him like this I recalled his pronouncement of yesterday: that he might be dead in little over a day. In the event, it appeared that he had not lasted even that long. Cautiously, I crossed the room and stood over his lifeless body, conscious of the flashing apparatus in the bedroom to my right. I knelt and felt for Cadwallader's pulse. His neck was clammy to the touch, the skin soft and loose. I had ascertained that there was no pulse when, to my horror, his flesh beneath my fingers began to sag. I jumped to my feet with a cry. As I watched, the length of his body subsided, deflated, and, as it did so, the face took on a puckered and warped expression. Only then did I notice the great rent in the writhing thing before me, an aperture in the epidermis that began at the chin and terminated at the abdomen. As the erstwhile Cadwallader shrivelled, the rent opened further to reveal a dark cavity within. I cried aloud again and backed off.

I was about to flee from the room when I heard, from the bedroom, a frail voice call my name. "Meredith," came the croak. "For the sake of humanity, come here!"

I hesitated, then squared my shoulders and plunged into the bedroom.

The first thing that caught my attention was the illuminated machine – the Temporal Equalizer, as he had called it. It stood upon a tripod of scimitar-shaped legs, silver in colour and ovoid in shape, with a collar about its middle from which the opalescent light emanated. A dozen levers bristled from its upper dome, and a series of buttons decorated its lower hemisphere. It stood about three feet high and hummed quietly to itself.

Then, after taking in this strange machine, I set eyes on the being which, until now, had passed itself off as Mr Cadwallader.

It sat slumped against the wall of the bedroom, a bipedal creature no larger than a five-year-old child. It was green and vaguely frog-like, and the stench that rose from it was odious in the extreme. It regarded me with crimson eyes the size of tennis balls.

"Meredith!" it gasped through a slit of a mouth. "Pull yourself together!"

I realised then that I was moaning to myself. I gestured to the sloughed skin in the outer room. "You... you...?"

"Of course!" it said impatiently. "Surely you realise that we Thallians could not resemble humans. 'Cadwallader' was a necessary disguise. My apologies for alarming you, but such was my fever I could no longer bear to be so confined. Enough of this! We rapidly approach the nodal point – the time of division is upon us. Listen carefully, Meredith, and do exactly as I say." He seemed to gather a deep breath, as if he were in great pain. "First, position yourself before the machine. Quickly, man!"

Part of me wanted to do nothing but run from the room and never return; but some other, eminently sensible part, held fast and obeyed the incapacitated Thallian.

"When the time arrives," he gasped, "take hold of the two longest levers and draw them towards you."

"But how will I know *when*?" I cried.

"It will be obvious! Once this is done, depress the seven green studs on the central collar, one by one with intervals of a second in between. Then return the levers to their original positions."

I grasped the levers in anticipation, my heart labouring. The frequency of the opalescent flashes accelerated, and with it the beat of my heart. On the floor, the alien took great breaths and regarded me through half-closed eyes.

There was a flash of lightning from outside, and the ship seemed to judder along its course as if buffeted by a mighty wave. Thunder clapped and the alien called: "Now, Meredith! Pull the levers now!"

With an involuntary cry I took a firmer grip on the rods and drew them towards me, and as I did so I realised why the alien required my assistance. The levers were stubborn; I had almost to hang onto them with all my weight in order to pull them into position. It was as if I were wrestling with the very spirit of the storm. As the levers came to rest, the air was instantly charged with a low, electric hum; outside, lightning flickered again. I depressed the green studs on the collar of the machine at the prescribed one second intervals, and it was as if each button controlled the stability of the climate outside. As each stud disappeared into the central collar, the severity of the storm increased; the thunder pealed ever louder and the lightning became nigh continuous.

"Now return the levers to their original positions!" the alien cried above the din of the storm.

This I did, but, if I expected the storm to cease then, I was disappointed. The turmoil continued unabated. Added to which, the entire ship was bathed in the eerie translucent glow, similar to that which emanated from the machine, and a high-pitched drone set my nerves on edge.

"Meredith," the alien called, "your work is almost over. The alignment is complete. All that remains is for you to do away with the evidence of my interference."

"In what way?" I shouted back.

"First, take the machine from the cabin, along with the Cadwallader suit, and throw them overboard. Hurry, and make sure you are unobserved!"

I did as he commanded. As the ship rolled from side to side, I hauled the device from the bedroom and across the floor of his cabin. I first ensured that the deck outside was deserted, and then dragged the contraption the rest of the way. I paused by the rail and took a grip on the midriff of the machine, hoisted it with all my strength and rolled it over the rail. I let go and watched it spin, still flashing and buzzing, down into the wind-whipped ocean. Then I went back for the rubber Cadwallader suit and, rather gingerly, carried the flaccid object to the side and dropped it overboard.

I returned to the bedroom, lighted now only by the flicker of lightning, and made out the small shape of the alien in the intermittent illumination.

"Help me to my feet!" he demanded.

Accustomed as I was to obeying his orders, I helped him upright. At the cold touch of his skin on mine, I shuddered with revulsion.

"Where to?" I cried.

He gestured feebly to the deck, and as we staggered from the cabin the steamer pitched and rolled in the storm. "And now?"

He fell against the rail and attempted to clamber overboard. I restrained him. "Are you insane!" I cried.

"I cannot be found on the Earth that remains in the past," he said. "And anyway, I am as good as dead already. Please, let me go!"

By now he had climbed upon the rail, and was balancing on the top-most bar. He turned his great crimson eyes on me. "Thank you, Meredith," he said, pulling his arm from my grip.

"But I must know," I cried, "*which Earth is this one?*"

He regarded me for what seemed like ages, then said, "I am afraid I cannot tell, Meredith. Only time will give you the answer."

And with that he released his grip on the rail and slipped overboard. With a cry of desperation I dashed forward, as if released from bonds, and stared after him. I beheld a quick glimpse of my friend's storm-tossed body before the ocean of Earth claimed him for ever.

As I sit here and finish this account, I am a man in the grip of fear. I alone, of all humanity, am aware of the cataclysmic change through which the planet passed this evening. I alone know that there exists, in time, two planet Earths – and two versions of myself! – and that one planet is doomed and the other destined to be saved by the intervention of an alien race.

The 'I' who writes this account might exist on the Earth doomed to self-destruction – or on the Earth destined to be saved by the Thallians.

There is, of course, one way I can find out for certain.

Oh, God, give me strength to leave the cabin and look into the night sky, to look upon *unfamiliar constellations of a future time* and know that it is *my* planet that has been saved...

THE TAPESTRY OF TIME

That spring, with winter well past and summer on the way, I decided that the time had come to visit Simon Cauldwell.

I had delayed our meeting for a number of reasons, some obvious, but others hidden in the depths of my psyche: fear, of course, was dominant. I didn't want to confront Cauldwell with my findings for fear of what I might learn.

I was forty-five, happily married with a ten-year-old daughter, and I held a secure post as a senior lecturer in archaeology at Oxford. I had reached the stage in my life at which I was confident that the future would hold no surprises. Perhaps I was complacent.

Fiona guessed that something was amiss. One evening in April she appeared at the door of my study. She must have been watching me for a while before I looked up and noticed her.

I smiled, tired.

"It's that skull, isn't it?"

I massaged my eyes. "What is?" I said, not for the first time amazed at my wife's perspicacity.

"Dan, ever since you found the thing, you've been different. Morose, withdrawn. If I believed in that kind of thing, I'd say it was cursed."

I managed to smile. "It's not cursed," I said. "Just misplaced. The skeleton was found with artefacts which date from a hundred years later."

She pushed herself from the jamb of the door and kissed the top of my head.

I said, "The paper I'm writing, trying to explain the anomaly, just isn't working..."

"I'm sorry, Dan. Dinner in ten minutes, okay?" She kissed me again and left the room.

Whenever I lied to Fiona, which wasn't often, I always wondered if she'd seen through me.

Misplaced artefacts, indeed...

The truth was far more perplexing, and worrying, than that.

A few days later I e-mailed Cauldwell, telling him that I'd had second thoughts about his offer.

He phoned later that afternoon. "Dan, so persistence pays off! You've seen sense at last. Good man. Look, when's convenient for you?"

"I'm free all this week."

"Excellent. Come over to the research station and I'll show you around the place. It's all hush-hush, of course. Top secret and all that."

"I understand," I said.

"Tomorrow at one suit? Excellent, see you then."

I replaced the phone, very aware of my thudding heartbeat. There was no turning back, now.

The headquarters of Sigma Research Inc. was buried away in the Oxfordshire countryside, miles away from the prying eyes of bustling Oxford.

I drove slowly through the tortuous, leafy lanes, considering my imminent meeting with Cauldwell and, despite myself, reviewing my dealings with the man. Despite the tone of bonhomie he had affected on the phone the day before, we had always been sworn rivals. Not to put too fine a point on it, I detested him.

He had been one of those old-fashioned academics ensconced in a sinecure at Oxford's richest and most conservative college. His resistance to theory, his inability to see the worth of research ideologically opposed to his own narrow views, had won him many enemies. Much to the surprise and envy of his colleagues, last year he had been head-hunted by Sigma Research, a big American outfit with a lot of dollars and a market-led excavation theory.

A few months after Cauldwell left Oxford, I discovered the eleventh century skull at a dig near the village of Sheppey, Herefordshire.

And a couple of days after that, Cauldwell himself phoned to invite me to join his team at Sigma Research. More than a little suspicious, I had told him I was quite happy at Oxford, thanks all the same.

Now I was following up his invitation – purely in the interests of research, of course.

Cauldwell met me in a plush reception area resplendent with thick crimson carpet and a jungle of potted-palms. It looked more like the foyer of a multi-national bank than the reception area of a private archaeological company.

He came smiling towards me, hand outstretched. "Dan, so pleased..."

Everything about him was big. He had a big, square head on big, wide shoulders. Even at college his dress had been eccentric: now he wore a loud shirt with a pattern *a la* Pollock, a pair of those ridiculous knee-length khaki shorts, and sandals from which his big, bare toes protruded obscenely.

He passed me a small plastic identity card bearing my name and a small photograph he'd obviously downloaded from the college website.

"Follow me. I'll give you the tour. You're privileged, of course. Not every Tom, Dick or Harry gets this. Just prospective employees."

I followed, not a little disgruntled at his assumption that I would be impressed.

He showed me into his office, a spacious area with few books but the latest computer technology.

What took my attention, however, was the plate glass window at the back of the room. It looked out over a big sunken chamber in which a dozen white-coated scientists were working at terminals.

He was saying, "I didn't know what research was till I began working for Sigma, Dan. I take it you read my last paper in *Historical Review*?"

I nodded. I had been impressed, despite myself.

Cauldwell smiled. "Groundbreaking, even if I do say so myself. Less to do with me than with the work of my team." He gestured through the glass at his 'team'.

I glanced at him. Such modesty was not usually his forté.

"Come, I'll show you the working end of the business."

He led me through a door and down a flight of steps into the sunken chamber.

Even at this stage, of course, I had my suspicions.

The chamber looked like the futuristic set of some sci-fi blockbuster: ranked computer terminals and banks of silver devices like lasers. At the far end of the room, however, and seeming out of place, was a tall, arched aperture that resembled nothing so much as a stained glass window.

I stared, surprised, for that was what I assumed it to be: a stained glass window, however inappropriate that might be in this secular setting.

Closer inspection revealed a rectangle of polychromatic tesserae, constantly shifting.

A woman in a white lab-coat came up to Cauldwell and passed him a small com-screen.

She smiled at me.

"Sally," I said. Would the surprises never end?

"Dan, fancy meeting you here."

"I was about to say the same."

Sally Reichs had been one of the finest post-grad students to come out of Oxford in years. By her mid-thirties, she'd written a couple of far-sighted books on her subject, the metallurgy of Anglo-Saxon Britain – and then disappeared from the scene.

Now I knew why. Head-hunted.

The odd thing was, she had professed an intense dislike of Simon Cauldwell while they were both working in the archaeology department at Oxford. More than once she had confided to me that she found his views, both professional and personal, detestable.

She must have seen my confusion. She gave me a look – a lop-sided, almost resigned smile – which signalled that she would tell me all at some point.

"Sal's quite brilliant," Cauldwell said as she returned to her terminal. "But of course you know that."

I ignored him and gestured at the multi-coloured screen at the far end of the chamber. A low hum, almost on the threshold of audibility, filled the air – along with what felt like a static charge.

I guessed, of course, but even then never really believed that my guess was correct.

We walked along an aisle between ranked terminals and paused beneath the aperture – it was perhaps three metres high – like supplicants.

Cauldwell said, "Did you wonder how I came to write such a revolutionary paper?"

I looked at him. "It wasn't quite what I've come to expect from you," I said.

He smiled at that. "Ah, I'll take that as a compliment."

A question caught in my throat. I was suddenly aware that I was sweating. "Tell me what's going on here," I almost pleaded.

Cauldwell nodded, not looking at me but staring at the shifting patterns on the surface of the screen. Seen closer to, the colours had about them the slick sheen sometimes seen on petroleum.

"What do you know about quantum physics, Dan?"

"Absolutely nothing," I admitted.

"Planck theory? Gupta's updating of Einstein?" He waved away my admission of ignorance. "No matter. Theory isn't required, merely the appreciation of the end result."

"Which is?"

He paused, then said, "Sigma Research has managed to break down the barriers that have hitherto prevented our access to other times."

He stopped there and looked at me, smiling. The word smug might have been coined to describe his self-satisfied expression.

"They do it with super-conducted tachyons and hyper-charged baryonic particles. I know, it doesn't make much sense to me, either. The result, at any rate, is a passage into the past, though never into the future. Once a month – as the expenditure of energy is prohibitively high – very briefly the portal is opened: three months ago onto 1050, last month 1052. We're going for 1054 in a few days from now."

I had known all along, of course. At least, I told myself as much. How else to explain the anomaly of the skull?

I considered telling Cauldwell abut my discovery, but something stopped me.

He was saying, "The only real problem, Dan, is that we can't open the portal to any time more than once. For the period of a year, the tachyon vectors specific to that time are seriously weakened and won't support passage. I mean, it would be wonderful to *revisit* specific times, but alas that's impossible."

I stared at him. "You mean, you actually visit, physically visit, these times?"

He nodded, smug again. "We do, though only for strictly allotted periods of up to thirty minutes. The power-drain, you see..."

I nodded, as if he had been explaining the cost of running an expensive car.

"At any rate, it would be superfluous to explain quite what a benefit to historical understanding this breakthrough has been..." Nevertheless, unable to pass up the opportunity for a lecture, Cauldwell proceeded to tell me all about his latest discoveries.

He conducted me around the chamber, interleaving his historical lecture with complex scientific explanations.

One hour later I found myself back in his office.

Over a coffee, Cauldwell said, "So, Dan, let me get to purpose of showing you around. Despite our differences, I respect your work. I think you could be a great asset to my team here at Sigma Research."

He passed a folder across the desk. "A contract. I think you'll find it more than a little enticing. Of course, I don't want an immediate answer. Go away and think about it for a few days. You have my number if you have any questions."

A little later, he rose and shook my hand.

I made to return the ID he had given me.

"Keep it, Dan," he said. "You'll need it, if you do decide to join the team."

I emerged into the bright summer sunlight not a little dazed – with a few questions answered, of course, while others remained tantalisingly opaque.

I drove slowly home, and decided that I would tell Fiona everything when I returned. It would help to talk, and her insight might shed light on aspects of the situation I was too blind to perceive.

That evening, over dinner, I told Fiona about my discovery of the skull and my subsequent investigations, then Cauldwell's showing me around the Sigma Research station and offering me a job.

She pushed her glass of wine aside and stared at me. "But... I mean, are you sure the bullet–"

I interrupted. "Of course I'm sure. The bullet passed through the left orbit and scoured a groove around the back of the skull. Death would have been instantaneous. The groove had aged over the centuries – it hadn't been made recently."

"But how would that be possible in the eleventh century? Perhaps it wasn't a bullet."

"It was. I found it lodged in the nasal cavity, eroded but recognisably a modern .02 bullet."

Fiona shook her head. "So this time-travel device at Sigma research... It must be connected, right? Someone goes back to that time – to, when was it, the 1070s? – and shoots dead some poor bloody innocent Anglo-Saxon..."

I massaged my eyes, wearily. "Fiona, there's more." I ordered my thoughts. "Although the skull dated from that time, circa 1070, it was the skull of a modern man."

"You aren't making sense, Dan!"

"It's upper jaw showed signs of contemporary dental work. A couple of fillings..."

Fiona nodded. "So it was someone from the research team who travelled back in time and was shot dead?"

"That's what happened. I made enquiries, accessed dental records. I found out who the skull belonged to."

She stared at me. "Whose was it, Dan?"

"Simon Cauldwell's," I said. "That isn't all," I went on. "I consulted a ballistics' expert, and from the bullet I found in the skull we identified the weapon used to kill Cauldwell."

She opened her mouth. I think she knew what was coming.

Last year, after a spate of violent robberies in the area, I had insisted that we purchase a pistol for the times when Fiona would be alone in the house.

"Not ours?" she said in barely a whisper.

I nodded. "Ours."

We went through all the possibilities over the course of the next hour or two. Did I kill Simon Cauldwell when I accepted the offered post and travelled back in time with him to the eleventh century? Why would I do such a thing? Granted, I didn't like the man – but I would never dream of shooting him dead.

And anyway, I had no intention of accepting his offer. Despite the amazing possibilities opened up by Sigma Research's temporal breakthrough, I could not see myself as some kind of Wellsian time-traveller.

But the fact remained – Cauldwell was shot dead, at some point in the eleventh century, with my pistol.

We went to bed late that night, and Fiona held me and made me promise that I would not take the Sigma post.

I promised... and tried to sleep, but my mind was full of temporal causality and paradox, and I passed a fitful night.

~

Fiona was out at yoga the following evening when the door-bell chimed.

I made my way from the study and pulled open the front door.

Sally Reichs stood in the April shower, looking determined. "Sally, what on Earth–?"

"I'm sorry. I had to see someone. It's important. I thought of you – I knew you'd listen." She stared at me, as if challenging me to deny her access.

"Of course, come in."

Bemused, I led her through the house to my study and sat her in the leather chair behind my desk. "Can I get you something? Coffee? Something stronger?"

"You don't happen to have a brandy?"

"On its way."

I fixed a double Remi Martin in the lounge, and one for myself. While there, I considered Sally's presence – it had to be connected to what was going on at Sigma, surely?

Sally was drying her face with a tissue. She took a breath, composing herself.

I sat on the armchair beside the desk and said, "Now, how can I help?"

"I can't confide in friends. They'd hardly believe me if I told them about happening. Then I thought of you – Cauldwell's trying to recruit you, right?"

"He did ask if I'd like to join the team, yes."

"Don't!" Her vehemence was surprising. "I mean, you don't know what it's like. Cauldwell isn't sane–"

"Sally, slow down. Take it easy. Now, what do you mean?"

She took a deep breath. "I've been back with him on two sorties now, to 1050 and 1052. They were mainly reconnaissance, observation."

I nodded, amazed at my calm reaction to something so amazing as this casual talk of time travel.

"And?"

"He wants to conduct an experiment. He has a theory – something to do with causality. Quantum physics. String theory. I don't honestly understand, but he thinks that there's more to existence than just this reality. He thinks that this world is one of an infinite number of similar worlds, and that every event in history somehow creates new, divergent time-lines – in effect, new realities, new worlds."

I vaguely recalled watching an episode of Horizon about something similar, though it had gone way over my head at the time.

"And Simon intends...?" I began.

Sally nodded. "He wants to do something back there that would prove the theory one way or another. Maybe introduce an invention, something the Anglo Saxons didn't have back then. I don't know... But, you see, I'm afraid that if he does go through with it..." She paused there, staring at me. "If he did this, and it changed things... Christ, I can't work it out. If he did change things, would that mean *we'd* be changed, *this* reality? Or would it mean that we'd simply go on as before, but that another reality would spring into existence, diverging from his intervention in the eleventh century?"

I stared at her, my head spinning. "If his theory of multiple realities is correct, then his intervention would merely create just another reality. But if he's wrong, if there's only *one* reality..." I pressed my temple, trying to work through the logic, "then wouldn't that mean that if he did make a change, then things would change *here*, too?"

Sally smiled. "But if his intervention back then changed the future, our present – then possibly Sigma Research might never come into being. But then how would he have been able to travel back to make the change!"

"The irresolvable paradox," I murmured.

"But do you see why he has to be stopped? If there is only one reality, and he changes it… then who knows what chaos he might wreak on our time."

I said, "Tell the high-ups at Sigma, okay? They won't let him go through with it."

"Yes. Yes, I'll do that. We're activating the interface to 1054 tonight, at midnight. I'll talk to someone before we go."

I fetched Sally another brandy, and once again we went through the mind-bending complexities of the situation. Towards ten o'clock, as she made to leave, I urged her again to confide in her superiors at Sigma.

At the door she gave me a quick hug, then ran out into the rain.

I watched her scarlet Renault speed into the night and made my way back to the study. I fixed myself another brandy and sat for an hour, going over what Sally had said and trying to untangle the convoluted skein of paradox with which she had presented me.

I should have made the connection earlier, of course. Perhaps the alcohol had dulled my senses.

Belatedly, I stood and crossed to the bookshelf where, next to the skull, I had kept the pistol.

It was not there, of course. In the time I had taken to fetch Sally a brandy, she had seen the pistol…

I hurried from the house and drove away at speed, though I knew the pursuit was futile. Sally had more than an hour on me, and, anyway, wasn't Simon Cauldwell's death pre-ordained, a fact ineluctably woven into the tapestry of time?

I reached the Sigma Research station at twenty minutes after midnight.

~

I flashed the ID Cauldwell had given me at the bored security guard on reception and made my way into the chamber.

The scene through the interface stopped me in my tracks.

The portal framed a vivid sunrise over rolling hills, with a wattle-and-daub village in the middle-ground. As I watched, transfixed, the scene shimmered like a heat haze.

"They should be back by now," a technician called.

I walked forward, unnoticed by the white-coated staff who had their attention on more pressing matters. We gazed up at the shimmering scene as if in awe.

"Communication's down!" someone called. "We've lost contact. If they don't get back..." she left the sentence unfinished.

"I can't hold it any longer! It's going!"

"They knew how long they had out there!" someone cried in despair.

The scene flickered, then. It stuttered like the image on a silent movie. It stabilised for a few seconds, showing the pristine, bucolic scene. Then the image winked out, to be replaced by the stained-glass effect of the interface in its deactivated phase.

The scene returned again – and I saw two small figures in the distance. They were standing face to face on a hillside perhaps a hundred metres away, and I judged that if they had moved themselves to sprint towards the interface they might have reached safety before the final shutdown.

But it appeared that they had other concerns. They faced each other in obvious confrontation, gesticulating: one figure moved forward, attempted to grab the other. Sally backed away, gesturing.

She reached for something in her jacket–

And the interface closed for the very last time.

The aperture could not be opened to exactly the same period, of course: no miraculous rescue of the time-travellers could be affected, for now.

A technician tried to calm his colleagues. He said that in the morning they would attempt to open the portal to the closest time possible to 1054, which would be 1056.

He was confident that Cauldwell and Reichs would be awaiting salvation...

Only I knew that only Reichs would be waiting.

I was wrong, as it happened.

Sally Reichs never returned to the twenty-first century. The disappearance of Cauldwell and Reichs was reported in the Oxford papers, briefly picked up by the national dailies, and then quietly forgotten.

Later that year I read that Sigma Research was closing its British base and relocating to the States, and I assumed that that would be the end of the affair.

A year after their disappearance, I received a call from my deputy at the dig near Sheppey.

They had, she said, made a truly astounding discovery.

I drove out to the site in record time, and beheld with wonder the shallow pit which cradled the skeleton of a woman judged to be in her seventies – old for the Middle Ages.

And the truly astounding discovery?

In a clay amphora wedged beside the corpse was a crude parchment scroll, covered in minute hand-writing.

The script, of course, was in contemporary English.

The following night I sat with Fiona in the conservatory, drank a glass of red wine and read a copy of Sally Reichs' eleventh century journal.

I stared through the conservatory window and considered Sally Reichs. I tried to decide if she was a fool or a hero, whether she had unjustifiably killed Simon Cauldwell on irrational grounds, or if her premeditated murder had indeed saved the future from some unknowable chronic catastrophe...

I have had a long and happy life, I read. I did what I had to do, I believe, and then found people I came to trust and love. I could have returned to the hillside, perhaps, and ventured home... but after two years in this age I had discovered something... someone... important to me.

But let me begin at the beginning, in a time far removed from this one...

THE FROZEN WOMAN

I was about to start work on an article for the local free paper when the phone rang.

"Amy Sullivan?" a male voice asked.

"Yes."

"Amy Sullivan, the journalist?"

"That's me," I said, though the title journalist was something of a misnomer these days. I waitressed at the local wholefood restaurant between commissions, which was most of the time.

"I represent Timothy Masters," he said. And left it at that.

The name was familiar. I recall wondering where I'd heard it before. A minor TV celebrity? A local musician yet to make it big? But why would Master's representative contact me?

Then the penny dropped. "Oh, my God," I said.

"Mr Masters would like to meet you."

"Me?" I said, incredulous.

"You and no one else but you. He's currently staying at Dudley manor in Shropshire. If you could get here for three this afternoon."

"Of course," I said, more than a little bemused. He gave me directions to the place, then rang off.

For years I'd been waiting for a break, an article or feature accepted by one of the nationals. Of late I'd come to accept that I'd never amount to anything more than a provincial hack.

And then, out of the blue, Timothy Masters contacts me.

Timothy Masters, the Frozen Man.

Dudley manor was a seventeenth century stately home set amid rolling parkland and extensive beechwoods. I made the hundred mile cross-country journey in a little under two hours, wondering all the way what Masters might want with me.

Perhaps twenty cars and a BBC outside-broadcast van were parked bumper to bumper in the long driveway. I left my beat-up VW Golf at the end of the drive and began walking. A posse of journalists and reporters kicked their heels outside the manor's imposing façade.

Before I reached them, a man in a blue suit apprehended me and said, "Ms Sullivan? If you'd care to come this way..."

I followed him around the side of the manor, but not before we'd been seen by a couple of the more eagle-eyed reporters. They gave chase.

"What do you know about Masters?"

"What has the Frozen Man said about his experience?"

Blue Suit hurried me through a side door and closed it firmly in the faces of our pursuers.

Without a word he led me through the manor. I took in plush-carpeted corridors, walls hung with what looked like Turners and Constables.

I thought of a question. "Can you tell me what Masters is doing here?"

The man paused in his purposeful striding. "Masters worked in the garden of the manor before his... his affliction, shall we say? Lord Dudley saw to his hospital care. He's a guest here until his recovery is complete."

Altruistic Lord Dudley, I thought. Or did his Lordship have an eye for the benefits that might accrue from harbouring the Golden Goose?

The man indicated a door. "After you."

We passed into a vast drawing room. To the left, a pair of French windows stood open, admitting a fragrant summer breeze.

Two men stood before the door, looking out. I recognised one of them, from his frequent TV appearances, as Lord Dudley.

The other, a grey-haired man in his fifties, introduced himself as William Grant, Timothy Masters' legal representative. It was to Grant I had spoken on the phone that morning.

Lord Dudley gave me the once-over, obviously wondering why Masters had demanded to see me, a worn-out, overweight thirty-something who couldn't even afford a decent wardrobe.

I was just as intrigued.

"Masters said nothing other than he wants to see you," Lord Dudley said. "As soon as he... ah... came round, he mentioned only your name."

I asked the question that had been bothering me for hours. "And why does he want to see me?"

Grant gestured through the French windows. "You can ask him that yourself."

A long, enclosed garden stretched away into the distance, all topiaried hedges, immaculate flowerbeds and gravel pathways. Perhaps fifty yards away, on a bench beside an ornamental fish pond, I made out a seated figure.

I took a hesitant step from the house, overcome then with a sudden apprehension.

I looked back. The three men were watching me. Grant gestured me on. I left the manor and walked along the path towards the Frozen Man.

I'd read about Masters, of course, as had just about every other literate citizen in the world.

Almost a year ago, while strolling down the aisle of a supermarket in Shrewsbury, Masters had stopped in the act of reaching out for a can of baked beans.

Stopped.

And never completed the move. Never, though it was hard to believe, started up again.

At first, wary shoppers suspected some in-store promotion. A mime artist employed by Sainsbury's or Heinz.

But there was something uncannily static about the man that frightened onlookers, they later reported.

Eventually, two store managers approached the man, moving around him, so the story went, as if he might be booby-trapped.

Then one of them reached out and touched Masters outstretched arm, and quickly withdrew his hand. Masters was cold, freezing cold. Other, braver souls approached, reached out, were amazed.

Then a particularly brazen youth pushed Masters in the chest, and he toppled.

The small crowd that had gathered by then sprang back, as if expecting the fallen man to shatter. Apparently he went down like a shop-window dummy, maintaining his rigid, standing posture with his arm outstretched even when lying on his back in the aisle.

He was taken away in an ambulance, admitted to the nearest general hospital, and examined thoroughly. It seemed that the Frozen Man, as he soon came to be known, was not actually frozen at all. He was coated in a substance impervious to probes, hard, almost chitinous – and unknown to modern science. He was still alive – CAT scans showed evidence of neural activity – but the medics could do nothing to revive him.

Timothy Masters had been no one special, until then. A gardener who worked on Lord Dudley's Shropshire estate. Single, thirty, with no relatives or family.

The story soon made the national news, and then was picked up by the international agencies. Timothy Masters' singular condition was something of a nine-day wonder. As time wore on, and he remained in his rigid, frozen position, media interest waned.

He remained in a private hospital for the next year, monitored by specialists and dusted down by the daily staff from time to time.

And then he came round. One morning two weeks ago a cleaner saw him move his hand, as if withdrawing it from the shelf he'd reached towards almost a year ago.

The woman had screamed and fled the room.

Media interest was intense again, with every journalist in the country, and beyond, wanting in on the story.

And Masters, for some unknown reason, had told his representative that he wished to see me, and only me.

I had never met Masters. Until he froze, I had never heard of him. I was not related to him, even distantly. My journalistic work cannot have been known to him. There was absolutely no reason why Masters should want to see me.

So naturally I was apprehensive, and intrigued, and bemused, as I hesitantly approached him in the ornamental garden of Dudley manor.

He turned as I crunched gravel. He smiled and gestured to the place next to him on the bench. "Amy, it's good to see you. Please, sit down."

I sat, quickly. How to describe my reaction to this perfect stranger?

He was dark, rather ordinary-looking, with kind eyes and a calm, reassuring smile. He radiated peace and a gentleness I associated more with followers of Buddhism.

He was watching me intently, and tears appeared in his eyes and slipped down his cheeks.

I let out a breath and laughed. "I don't understand. This is ridiculous. I've never met you before in my life. I don't know you from Adam!" I think I was a little hysterical, and at the same time excited.

I looked at him. "What do you want?"

He reached out and took my hand. His own hand was warm. I felt not in the least threatened by his sudden intimacy: it seemed entirely natural.

"Amy, what do you believe?"

I let out a breath. I can't claim to have been expecting any particular question, but this one had me stumped.

"I... Well – I don't quite know..." I stared into his eyes. Blue, gentle, compassionate.

I shrugged and said, "I'm not religious. I suppose you could call me a wishy-washy liberal humanist." I laughed. "I give money to Greenpeace and Friends of the Earth, but I'm not a member of any political party."

He squeezed my fingers. "We don't know anything," he said, with a quiet authority that silenced me. "Oh, we think we do. We take in the world and make our assumptions and listen to the experts and form views and opinions, but it's all really so much conjecture. I mean, consider the world-view of a goldfish in a pond." He pointed towards the bulbous koi mooning around in the water before us. "What do they know?"

"I'm sorry... I don't understand."

He smiled. "I'll tell you," he said.

"Why me?" he said. "I was no one special, the head gardener at Dudley. I'd studied horticulture and land-management at Pershore, and worked for Lord Dudley for the past nine years. Then one day in Sainsbury's I reached out and..."

"What happened?"

"I thought I'd died. I felt an intense heat all over my body. I thought I'd had a heart attack and gone to... well, I thought I was in Heaven. At first. There was no pain, just a wonderful sense of peacefulness. I was surrounded by a golden light, and yet I had the feeling that I'd travelled a long, long way. Then I looked around and saw *them*, and I panicked. I experienced terror, a fear I had never known before..." He stopped, his gaze distant.

I had to prompt him. "Them?" I asked.

"The beings," he said. "They were all around me, examining me. I was naked."

"Beings?" I echoed. "Alien beings?" A shiver passed down my spine.

"Not aliens. Humans. But humans vastly different from you or me. I was in what looked like a park. I stood in a glade, and all around me were these... beings. I panicked. I lashed out, yelling. Then one of the creatures reached out and touched me, and I lost consciousness.

"When I came round again, I was lying on a padded surface under a silver awning, a kind of pavilion overlooking the glade. There were fewer of the creatures watching me.

"They told me not to fear them. Except... they didn't talk to me. I heard words in my head. They told me that, for a time, they had feared for my health, so severe had my reaction been to the transference."

"The transference?"

"That's what they called it. They were slight creatures, with larger heads than you or me, and tiny features. I asked who they were, and they told me."

He stopped. He turned his head to look at me, and something in his eyes, a kind of burning veracity, told me that he, at least, believed the truth of what he had experienced.

He went on, "They said that two million years had elapsed since my time, and that they were our descendants." He smiled. "And I accepted that. I believed them. It seemed so obvious. They reassured me that I would come to no harm, and that they would return me, in time."

"They wanted to study you?" I asked.

What did I believe? Did I truly think that evolved humans had plucked Timothy Masters from the twenty-first century and whisked him two million years through time, in order to study him? I don't honestly know.

"I asked them what they wanted with me, why they had brought me there. They said they were scientists, and wanted to observe me. They were curious about their ancestors. They wanted to know how I worked, how I reacted to stimuli. They told me that I would remain here for a time, but that I would not be alone. They said they would provide me with someone I could love." He stopped and looked at me.

I think I knew, then, what was coming next.

He said, "I received the impression that their kind no longer loved, that perhaps it was no longer a biological necessity for the people of the far future. They said that they were affecting the transference of a woman, and that when I awoke I would no longer be alone. One of their number reached out to touch me, and I lost consciousness."

He squeezed my fingers. "And when I came awake again, you were standing on the grass beneath the silver awning, watching me."

I was prepared, as I said. I knew what had been coming. It made a kind of crazy sense – the reason he had summoned me here.

But I shook my head. "Impossible!"

"The beings were no longer visible," Masters went on, "though I sensed their presence. I stepped forward and embraced you. It was as if... as if I had been waiting all my life for this moment. It was right, we belonged. We fitted. However, at the same time, I knew that the beings had manipulated this, that they had somehow brought about this attraction, this feeling of love that overwhelmed me."

I bridled. "And what about me?" I asked. "Did you consider my feelings at all?"

He smiled and squeezed my hand again. "As amazing as it seems, you felt the same."

I pulled my hand away. For a brief, crazy second it came to me that this was a set-up: I had been lured here against my will for some bizarre purpose... But how could that be? Had Masters staged his own freezing?

I said, "And I wasn't in the slightest fazed at being whisked two million years through time, to be accosted by a stranger? I wasn't terrified?"

He was shaking his head. "Of course not."

"Of course not?" I repeated, incredulous. "How can you say that?"

"Because," he said, "you knew where you were. And I was no stranger."

I was close to tears then. "I don't understand," I said.

"They were manipulating us," Masters said, "I knew that. I never again saw the beings while you and I were together, but I was always aware of their presence. We lived for years in a paradise. We ate fruit and drank from streams. We had no worries, and we were never bored, or concerned at what had happened to us. It was as if our past lives had been erased from our memories, as if we lived only for the day, and for each other. We were in love, and it was blissful."

I stared at him. "Years?" I said.

"So it seemed. We aged. We grew old. I came to understand what true love was, during that time. We grew old together, decrepit, but not once did my love for you diminish. We changed so incrementally over the years that I loved the old woman just as passionately as I had loved you when you first arrived."

I shook my head. The rationalist in me asked, "But we were there together? And yet you were frozen here while I wasn't..."

He smiled and touched my hand. "They transferred me first," he said. "I was an experiment, to see if they could accomplish the feat. Only then did they transfer you, from later in our own time."

"But why?" I asked. "Why not take me at the same time as they took you?" Then I was taken by the corollary of my acceptance of his story: at some point in the future, I too would undergo stasis, would freeze as the beings transferred me.

I tried to pull away, tell myself how preposterous all this was!

Masters said, "You died in that future age, Amy, and I grieved. The beings showed themselves again, and thanked me, and sent me back to warn you of what was to come. They did not want you to suffer the same terror that I had suffered. And of course, because you had come to me without fear, they knew I had returned successfully and met you here. A paradox of causality."

We sat in silence for a time. I removed my hand from his. I stared around the garden, at the fish in the pond. I was surrounded by normality, by the everyday we take for granted. I willed myself to disbelieve his story.

I turned to face him. "And," I said, "you expect me to believe everything you've said?"

He smiled. "I can convince you, Amy. You see, you told me all about yourself. I know your every secret."

I felt so terribly vulnerable, then. How dare this stranger claim such intimacy, on the pretext of such a bizarre story?

"You told me about your unhappy childhood, Amy. About the bullies. Your mother's death when you were thirteen, your father's depression. You told me about what happened when you were twenty-five—"

"Stop!"

"—what your lover did to you. You told me that you had never loved anyone since that time, never trusted anyone enough to love."

"Please stop," I begged.

He stopped, and held me. "Now do you believe?"

I asked at last. "Why us?"

"Why not us?" he said. "It had to be someone."

"What now?"

He touched my cheek. "You told me it was the day after you met me here, Amy. You returned home this afternoon, tried to finish your article." He laughed. "But you couldn't, of course. Then, in the morning, tomorrow at nine, after a sleepless night, you felt the heat, and you were transferred."

We stood, and held each other for a long, long time.

When I next looked at him, I saw that he was weeping. "Timothy?"

"You died up there," he said, "in the future. I watched you die, and I grieved. Then the beings sent me back." He sighed and stared at me. "I'm doing this for the *me* who was transferred, the person in the future. But do you realise how hard it is for the me of now, knowing that I might never again see you?"

I struggled for words. "But they sent you back..." I began. "Why not me?"

He shook his head, avoiding my eyes. "But I saw you *die* up there," he said.

I held him for a long time, and then I fled.

I returned to my flat, ignoring all the reporters encamped in the street. The phone rang continually. I turned down offers from three national papers for my story.

I raged. I wept for the life I had lost, however inadequate that life had been. I wept for my uncertain future.

I think I went a little mad.

I thought of the wasted years, and asked myself, again and again, how Masters might have known about what had happened on the night of my twenty-fifth birthday, when what should have been so good had turned so bad. Had I really told Masters, two million years into the future?

The idea was preposterous, of course. My sanity demanded that I disbelieve him.

I spent a sleepless night, just as he had said I would, and tried to come up with a rational explanation to account for the previous afternoon.

In the morning, approaching nine, I considered my life to date, the fear and unhappiness.

I stared at my old alarm clock on the bedside cabinet, not knowing what I wanted.

Nine o'clock came and went, and I was torn with relief, and at the same time a savage disappointment.

I stood and moved towards the bathroom.

And froze.

Froze.

Unable to move.

And then I felt the heat.

I stood beneath the silver awning, and he reached out for me, and we came together.

We lived a life as he had described it, our thoughts and sensations manipulated no doubt by the observing far future humans: like insects under glass, like koi carp in a pond, but no less happy for that fact.

I came to know Timothy as I had known no other as we aged together in paradise.

I told him about our meeting in the grounds of Dudley Hall, of which of course he had no memory. I told him that I had fallen in love with him then, against my better judgement. Was ours the strangest union of two humans, ever?

And much later I died. I recall his tortured expression as sleep claimed me, and I slipped away.

And came awake again in my own age, approximately a year after my departure.

I was in a room in Dudley manor, a sunlit room overlooking the ornamental gardens. I was quite alone, and felt a moment's panic at the fact of Timothy's absence. For so long we had been together.

I slipped out of bed and hurried to the window and stared out.

And there he was, standing in the garden below.

He was staring at the fish in the pond.

He turned, as if sensing my surveillance, then smiled and lifted an arm and moved towards the house.

CRYSTALS

I came to the island for a holiday at a time in my life when I was looking for a quiet retreat away from the pressures of life. That was ten years ago, and I live on the island to this day. The place gets to you that way. Besides, the mainland holds too many bad memories for me.

I first rented, and later bought, a small cottage overlooking the bay where the alien starship crashed twenty-five years ago. You can see the sleek rear fin projecting from the water like a scimitar at high tide; and at low tide a long stretch of the upper superstructure is visible.

Sometimes, when I've been drinking too much and thinking of the past, I just sit by the window and stare out at the golden ship, and try to visualise its voyage through the empty gulfs of space... The locals claim that every year the ghosts of the aliens gather at the hilltop graveyard where they are buried and make their way back to the submerged ship. But, sober or drunk, I've yet to see one of these extraterrestrial spectres, and I've spent many a lonely anniversary of the crashlanding staring out into the night.

Nowadays the starship is not the tourist attraction it once was. For the first few years after the ship's abrupt arrival, the island was the eighth wonder of the world. When the security forces allowed the evacuated islanders to return, and the dead aliens had been thoroughly examined and interred, millions of tourists flocked to the island. The starship was the subject of countless scientific probes and television profiles. A mini-city was constructed in the neighbouring bay to cater for the sightseers, and visitors camped on the headlands just to be closer to the evidence that life existed elsewhere in the universe. Now there are no more tents in the pastures, and the hotels and chalets along the coast stand empty and neglected. Visitors still make the occasional pilgrimage, but for the most part the starship's only admirers are the scientists who arrive each summer, hoping to discover something overlooked in the original investigations.

When I first came to the island, saturation coverage had had its effect. The starship was *passé*. Those who had lived with the crashlanding had had enough: wonders, however magnificent, are never quite the same to a generation reared with them. The island was rural and peaceful in a way that much of the mainland was not, and I decided that this was the place for me. Psychologists might have made something of the fact that I had fled London and a failing marriage to come to the one place on Earth where extraterrestrial life had, albeit accidentally, made itself known. It was only later, in my more drunken and maudlin lapses, that I came to identify with the alien hulk. We were both victims of fate, washed up alone and far from home. Later still, the wreck became quite simply a familiar landmark – safe and reassuring like all things familiar.

That afternoon, as I sat at my desk and made notes for a life of Beethoven I was working on for an educational publisher, my ex-wife was the person furthest from my thoughts. I had last heard from her shortly after our separation, in the form of a letter telling me that she had landed a lectureship at a large American university. She indicated that she intended to make a new life for herself and her daughter out there, and I assumed –

or rather hoped – that we would never meet again. A few years later an editor of our mutual acquaintance told me that he'd met her on a recent visit to the States, and that she had remarried.

It was around five and I was contemplating the first scotch of the day, as a prelude to some serious drinking later that evening, when the screen chimed.

I turned in my swivel chair and turned it on, presuming a call from Harrison. The picture flickered and, after a couple of false starts, expanded into life.

It wasn't Harrison. His face was large and bright red, not this evenly-complexioned mocha. Harrison was ugly, whereas the woman who smiled out at me was still beautiful, despite the passage of time; and Harrison didn't provoke from me the painful rush of memories I thought I'd managed to bury over the years.

I took a breath. "Parveen..."

"You look surprised to see me, Daniel."

"Where are you?" I searched the screen for the time indicator that accompanied all trans-atlantic calls, but the top right corner was blank.

"I'm in London, Daniel."

My stomach turned. "What do you want?"

"I'm here to see Sita settled into university–"

I felt something stick in my throat. "How is she?" I had never written regularly to Sita, but my letters had ceased altogether five years ago, when she was thirteen.

"She's very well, Daniel." She paused, then, watching me closely, said, "She would very much like to see you."

"I... I'm not sure about that."

"Don't worry. I'm staying in London. She'll be making the trip by herself."

I shook my head, speechless for a moment. Then, "Why...?"

She just stared at me, smiling.

I said, "Christ, you haven't told her, have you?"

"Of course not. We agreed on that, didn't we?"

I nodded.

Parveen went on, "But I think it's high time she was told, Daniel."

"And you want me to do it?" I asked.

She smiled at me, sweetly. "It would sound much better coming from you," she said. "You have a way with words, after all..."

Much better for who? I was tempted to ask.

I reached out and poured myself a drink. "Very well. Okay."

"She's often asked why you never visit her."

I just stared, amazed by her cruelty.

I said, "And you're not at all concerned about what she might think about you when I tell her the truth?"

"Sita and I are not as close as we once were, Daniel. She's eighteen now, an independent young woman with her own life."

"There's a ferry to the island at three tomorrow," I told her. "It gets in around four. Tell Sita I'll be waiting at the harbour." I reached out to cut the connection.

She saw the move and smiled to herself. "Aren't you going to ask me how I am, Daniel?"

"You look very well."

"I am. Very well. And you, Daniel? Did you ever remarry?"

I switched off the screen.

I poured myself another scotch, got up and stood by the window. After a minute, almost against my will, I took an old manilla envelope from the bottom drawer of my desk and shook out a dozen small snapshots. Sita, aged from three months to five years, when Parveen and I had separated. A chubby bundle in rompers... a pre-schooler in moonboots and a chunky parka... It was hard to imagine that she was eighteen now – a young woman. In the photographs, I could see the seeds of beauty in her dark brown eyes and thick jet hair.

The screen chimed again, but I was damned if I was going to allow Parveen to twist the knife even further. I ignored the summons and stared at the photographs.

Five minutes later, when the soft trilling started again, I dived at the screen, ready with an insult to make it plain that I resented her intrusion.

This time it *was* Harrison.

I slumped in my seat and raised my glass in salute.

He peered at me. "You don't look too well, Dan. Hitting the bottle already?"

"I'm fine. Good to see you."

"I suppose you've heard the news?"

I looked dumb and Harrison laughed. "Look through the window, Dan. Tell me what you see."

I shrugged, swivelled my chair. "The bay," I said. "The ship. There's a team of scientists working out there." In the gathering twilight I could see a string of lights marking the outline of the pontoon walkway stretching from the shore to the broad back of the starship. I'd watch the scientists going back and forth all day, a welcome distraction to the chore of making notes.

"That's 'em," Harrison said. "An outfit calling themselves Omni-Science. I've been meeting with the other residents all day. We're getting up a petition of protest."

"What on earth for?" I said. "Aren't they just another bunch of scientists?"

Harrison leaned forward, as if eager to join me in the room. "Listen, Dan. Just another bunch of scientists they might seem to you, but you don't know what I know."

"And what might that be?" I asked.

"What are you doing tonight?"

"Bloody stupid question."

"Good man. I'll see you around the usual time and tell you all about it then. Look after yourself, Dan." And he was gone.

I stared out at the lights, my smile at Harrison's eccentricity fading as my gaze fell to the snapshot on the desk. A five year-old Sita in Parveen's arms, both of them smiling out at me from a time far happier than now.

One of the things that had attracted me to the island, and had persuaded me to stay, all those years ago, was its stubborn insistence that change was not necessarily concomitant with the passage of time. This part of England remained forever becalmed in the '90s of the last century. Many residences were still linked by old-style telephones, and village shops still catered to the needs of the islanders. The people, too, were old-fashioned. They were friendly enough, but kept to themselves, which suited me fine.

The Blue Man, despite its name, was the building that had changed least over the years. The actual walls of the building dated from the sixteen-hundreds, and the interior furnishings were of the oak beam and horse-brass variety so beloved of cliché.

Harrison was waiting for me by the roaring fire. He was the only local I had allowed myself to get to know in all my time here. He was a stocky ex-banker who had retired to the island after the death of his wife, and we had found ourselves thrown together through mutual loss and a taste for good whisky.

"So what's all this rubbish about Omni-Science?" I asked him.

He regarded me with a bleary eye. "I wish it were rubbish, Dan. I'd sleep a lot better if that were so. If you still think it's rubbish when I've finished, go talk to Hendry and the others over there." He nodded towards a gaggle of locals at the bar, talking animatedly amongst themselves.

"I'm all ears," I said, taking a sip of Glenfiddich.

"Omni-Science–" and he pronounced the title with derision "–intend to raise the starship."

I sat up. "Hasn't that been proposed before? I thought it'd been looked into and declared impossible."

"And so it was, twenty years ago. Since then they've developed new techniques. Remember the Titanic? Well, they plan to do the same thing with the starship. Raise it and tow it over to the mainland."

I nodded, let the silence stretch, and then said, "So what's your objection?" I had become accustomed to having the starship on my doorstep, and I'd miss its familiarity. But we'd soon get over the removal of our sole claim to fame.

"My objection," Harrison said, "is that they plan to demolish half the island in the process."

That night a force eight gale raged across the straits and pounced on the island. As I lay awake, listening to the noisy assault on the cottage, I secretly hoped it would continue and so make the ferry crossing tomorrow unfeasible. Towards dawn, however, the wind ceased. I got up then, unable to sleep, and set out on a long walk around the bay.

The day was ice-cold and winter-bright. The sun fell in great searchlights from a raft of flat-bottom cumulous out over the shipping lanes, and a bitter wind blew between the headlands. Sunlight caught the rearing fin of the starship, winking a golden semaphore. The storm had wrought havoc to more than just the odd tree uprooted along the coast. The pontoon walkway, connecting ship to shore, was a tangled mass of wreckage. A couple of juggernauts had pulled up on the bay road and a dozen Omni-Science personnel were attempting to salvage what was left of the construction. I wondered if the storm were an omen of things to come.

One hour after setting out, my head full of Parveen and her betrayal, I arrived back at the cottage. I was crossing the beach when I saw half a dozen black nodes scattered along the high-tide line of seaweed and driftwood. I knelt and picked one up. It was as black as coal, but crystalline in structure – a thing of remarkable beauty. As I gripped it in my hand, I fancied that I felt a slight warmth emanating from its faceted surface. I slipped it into my coat pocket and stood, holding it as a talisman against the cold wind. I had hoped that the physical exertion of the walk would take my mind off the day ahead, but the exercise had served only to concentrate my thoughts. Today I would be meeting Sita again for the first time in nearly twelve years, and it was my duty to tell her the unpalatable truth... Against my will, I thought back over the years to that period of unhappiness, and cursed Parveen for it.

Then I returned inside, made myself a coffee and stared at the jet crystal. For the rest of the day I tried to concentrate, unsuccessfully, on the life of Ludwig van Beethoven.

I left the cottage just before four and drove around the island to the ferry terminal.

I parked across the street from the quaint weatherboard building through which the arrivals would pass when they ferry docked. There were a few other cars parked up, and the island's only taxi waiting for trade. I climbed from the car and nervously watched the hover-ferry approach the harbour wall. I thought back a day and realised that, but for my ex-wife's call, I would be safe and warm in the cottage now, not out here with my stomach clenched in a sickening knot of fear.

Five minutes later the passengers came down the steps from the terminal building in ones and twos. Sita emerged and paused; then she saw me and waved hesitantly. I walked over to meet her.

She wore a long black coat with a high collar, and loose cavalier boots. She carried herself with a poise and assurance that I recognised, with a painful sense of *déjà vu*, as belonging to Parveen at the age of twenty.

She lowered her suitcase to the ground and embraced me. When she pulled away and swept a strand of hair from her face, there were tears in her eyes. "It's good to see you again, dad. You've hardly changed. I recognised you immediately." She spoke softly, with a slight American accent.

"You've changed so much," I told her. "Here, let me take that." I found it hard to meet her gaze, and I felt the distance that they years had put between us. The brief respite of stowing her suitcase in the boot, while Sita settled herself in the passenger seat, allowed me to take a mental breath before plunging in again.

"So..." I said with false cheer as I started the engine. "I hear you're starting university over here."

"I start at Cambridge next week. Girton." She stopped there, allowed the silence to expand uncomfortably, and then said, "Why didn't you come over to see me, dad?" It was an accusation.

I made a needless performance of checking the rear-view mirror before overtaking a tractor. "I'm sorry... I just thought it best if I didn't. I know your mother didn't want to see me again. It would have been difficult."

"I thought of you every day," she said in a whisper.

I experienced a sudden and incisive hatred of my ex-wife then. "How is your mother?" I asked. "I heard she remarried."

"She's as well as ever," Sita replied. Then, "I don't know whether I dislike her husband because he came between mother and me, or because he tried to replace you..." She said this with a quiet matter-of-factness, an acuity beyond her years.

I changed the subject. "What will you be studying at Cambridge?" I asked.

"Genetics. Cellular engineering. I'd really like to do some research eventually on the plants they found on Titan last year."

"What do you want to do when you graduate?" I felt safe on the neutral territory of her future.

"By that time... who knows? We might even have found the homeplanet of the little Blue Men. I'd love to work in space. That's where the future is."

"The crashlanding certainly boosted NASA's credibility," I said, for want of an original observation.

"This island put space on the map!" Sita laughed.

"I expect you're looking forward to seeing the starship?"

"That's the only reason I came here, dad." She said this with a mischievous grin that I recognised from her infancy. "Is it far from your place?"

"My cottage overlooks the bay where the ship came down. I have a grandstand view."

It was dark by the time we arrived. The moon had not yet risen and a swift cloudrace covered the stars. All that could be seen of the starship's superstructure were the reflections from the lights on the reconstructed walkway. I promised Sita that we'd take a closer look in the morning.

I fixed a meal – over the years I had become a passable cook – and as we ate, our inconsequential chatter breaking the ice of earlier, I realised that this was the first time during my occupancy of the cottage that I'd entertained a woman to dinner.

By nine that evening, when we entered the warmth of the Blue Man, I felt that I had come to know Sita a little better. She was similar to how Parveen had been in her twenties, but more intelligent, more caring, and she had a sense of humour totally lacking in my ex-wife. There was still a certain distance between us, but I knew the reason for that. Sita still resented me – and no doubt could not understand my reasons – for not visiting her over the years.

On any other night Sita's entry might have turned a few heads – on account of both her colour and her good looks – but tonight the snug was empty: all the patrons were packed into the back room.

Harrison saw me and came out briefly as I stood at the bar. He noticed Sita seated by the fire and smiled at me. I think I once mentioned, long ago, that my wife and daughter were living in the States.

I carried our drinks over to the table. "Harrison, meet Sita. Sita, this old reprobate is Harrison. My faithful drinking companion."

He took her hand with old-world charm. "Delighted to make your acquaintance, Sita."

She smiled, and then nodded towards the hubbub in the back room. "What's going on in there?"

"A meeting. Council of war, don't you know. We've brought down a lawyer from London." He glanced at his watch." In fact, it's just about to start. Won't you join us?"

"I'll catch up with what happened later," I told him.

Harrison excused himself with a bow towards Sita and hurried off.

She sipped her drink. "A council of war about what, exactly?"

I told her about Omni-Science's plans to raise the starship.

She said, "Omni-Science is big. When they say they intend to do something, they usually do it."

"And demolish half the island in the process," I told her. "Harrison was explaining it to me last night." I outlined Omni-Science's plans.

One of the main difficulties in moving the starship, other than its obvious weight and size, was the fact that it had suffered major structural damage when it crash-landed. Otherwise Omni-science would have simply filled it with air and towed it across to the mainland. What they planned to do instead was to drain the bay, encase the ship in a massive frame of girders, and haul in up the hillside – incidentally demolishing my cottage in the process. Then they planned to remove the eastern headland, bring in an enormous platform and place the starship on top of it. Only then could it be towed with ease across the straits to the mainland. We would be compensated, of course – there was even talk of rebuilding the headland – but the locals were sceptical.

Sita heard me out, then said, "But don't you think it would be a small sacrifice to make for the possible benefits to science? I'm sure the experts will find a lot more of interest and probable value when they study the ship at close quarters."

"*Possible* benefits, *probable* value. Can you guarantee that anything will come from the removal?"

She shrugged. "Even if there's no direct scientific breakthrough, the ship will be on show in its entirety for the first time. It will stir up the public's interest in space all over again. And you'll have your compensation."

"Perhaps it's the disruption I'm afraid of," I said, guiltily. "I've had it easy for so long, fallen into a rut. Do you know, I haven't left the island in almost seven years?"

"You're getting old," she jibed. "Where's your ambition?"

I laughed. "It's fine for someone of your age to talk about ambition. When you're as old as I am..."

"Mother's your age. She's still ambitious. She has her sights set on a professorship at Princeton." She stopped suddenly, realising her mistake, and stared into her martini.

"You're so like your mother, Sita. I remember when I first met her – she was a year older than you are now. And so full of ambition. Somewhere along the way she left me standing. Perhaps that was what..." I stopped myself. "Did I ever tell you that I once planned to write the best English novel of the century?"

Before I became too maudlin, the meeting in the back room adjourned. The islanders filed out. On his way to the bar, Harrison gave me the thumbs down.

Sita took my hand. "I can't begin to tell you how much I've missed you. Letters and e-mails weren't enough. When I got the scholarship, the first thing I thought was that I could see you again regularly."

"Sita..." I was tipsy enough to tell her then, but I could see from her smile that she was happy, thinking about the future, and I couldn't bring myself to hurt her with the truth about the past.

In the morning I knew it had to be today.

Sita woke me early and demanded that I take her to see the starship. After breakfast we left the cottage and walked around the bay. Sita wore her cavalier boots and a crimson ski-jacket, and when she put her arm through mine and leaned into the wind I was immediately transported back to the time we had taken long walks, summer and winter, in Hyde Park. Following the joy of this memory came the sudden, stabbing sadness.

I explained that we would get a better view of the starship from the elevated position of the western headland. We struggled up the worn, sandy path, Sita tugging me after her when the incline defied my stamina. At the top we stood side by side and stared down at the bay.

The tide was out and the great golden curved back of the ship dazzled in the winter sunlight. The superstructure was engraved in a baroque pattern of scrolls and whorls – and it was this artistry, as well as the beauteous aesthetics of the ship, that helped give the impression of *otherness*. I tried to imagine NASA giving over one of their craft to artists at the design stage of production.

Sita gasped and laughed.

Omni-Science had increased their activity in the area: all manner of technological apparatus littered the shoreline. I noticed that the calm surface of the bay had been divided into a neat grid pattern by lines of white tape stretching from shore to shore. In many of these squares, divers worked from platforms, jumping backwards into the cold sea and disappearing in a surge of bubbles. As we watched, small figures crossed the pontoon walkway and strode along the starship's broad promenade, like birds on the back of a great basking whale. More divers entered the ship through gaps and rents in the scroll-work to investigate the dark interior.

All this did not go unopposed. On the foreshore in front of an Omni-Science juggernaut a crowd of locals had gathered, led by the stocky figure of Harrison. They waved banners and placards and tried to engage the scientists in dialogue.

"I should really be down there with them," I said.

Sita nodded and squeezed my arm. "And I should be with the scientists."

We laughed and retraced our tracks from the summit. Halfway down I stopped and said, "What on earth are they doing?"

The islanders had left the road and formed an excited mob on the beach. One of their number shouted something, and a group of scientists joined the protestors. Something was handed over, which the scientists examined and passed around. Many islanders were searching the sand, bending down and picking things up and passing them to their neighbours. A scientist called a halt to the diving, beckoned the workers on the back of the ship to join them.

Then, much to my amazement, the scientists and islanders were shaking hands, in one or two cases even embracing. I stared in disbelief. It was as if armistice had been declared and the opposing forces were suddenly one.

"Come on!" Sita said. She pulled me after her and we hurried down the hillside.

The scientists and islanders had come together on the beach, perhaps twenty or thirty in all, and they seemed drugged. They wore inane smiles like addicts on ecstatic highs. Whoops and yelps of laughter went up from joyous individuals, both stranger and local alike.

Then I saw the cause of their odd behaviour.

The beach was strewn with the same black crystals as the one I had picked up the other morning. People were holding these and tripping. Sita knelt and picked one up. An expression of indescribable wonderment transformed her features. "Sita?"

Harrison staggered up to me. "Dan, this is incredible! The storm must have washed them ashore the other day – they're from the ship." He thrust a crystal into my hand.

And I was suddenly overcome with his joy.

"There's two kinds, Dan. Blank ones that can be imprinted with emotions like that one, and others which have already been used – *which the aliens have used!*"

He thrust another one at me, and I understood.

I felt as if a low current of electricity were flowing through me, and into my head came the fantastic visions of far stars and alien civilisations. I was in contact with the thoughts and emotions of the Blue Man who had used this crystal. These came as rushes of great joy and tragedy – universal constants, seemingly – and visual scenes as clear as my own memories. I picked up other crystals and discovered that the ship had been a colony vessel from a distant star on the edge of our galaxy, that their mission had been to locate habitable planets and intelligent aliens...

As the crystals circulated amongst us I received ones which had been blank when first picked up, but which were imprinted now with the sheer delight and surprise of the individuals who had found them. I experienced other peoples' joy, matching my own, at the magnitude of the discovery and what it meant.

Later, hours later perhaps, I forced myself away from the gathering and hurried back to the cottage. Sita was still out there, lost in visions of alien wonder. She would be gone for a good while yet.

The crystal was still on the desk where I had left it.

I recalled the mood I had been in the day before when I had found it – and when I picked it up now the pain and regret returned to me, intensified. Beyond the pain, the crystal had recorded the reason I had felt that way. I had held the alien stone for a matter of minutes, yet now I could sit with it for hours, reliving the past.

Into my mind's eye swam the face of Parveen as she told me that Sita – whom I had loved as my own for eight years – was the daughter of an associate of hers; she had planned to marry him, and would have, had it not been for his death in a yachting accident a matter of weeks before Sita's birth.

With these visions, I relived again the mixed emotions of love and hate, and the painful decision to leave my wife and Sita and come to the island. For months I had agonised over this, and argued and reasoned with Parveen, but it was obvious that she no longer felt anything for me, and had not for a long time – and all this was revealed in the crystal with an intensity I found hard to take.

As I sat at the desk and grasped the crystal, it came to me that this was the only way to inform Sita of her mother's betrayal.

She came back an hour later. She crossed the room and hugged me.

"The scientists might not need to move the ship now," she said. "They've found crystals containing details of the aliens' science and technology." She was flushed and exuberant from the cold wind and the excitement of the discovery, and as she smiled at me I realised that I hadn't felt an all-consuming love like this towards anyone for a long, long time.

"Sita," I said, feeling the crystal in my hand, communicating all my pain.

I almost passed it to her then, but stopped myself.

The crystal was *too* truthful, of course. When I came to tell her that she was not my daughter, I would do so without all the pain and bitterness. I wanted Sita to love her mother, and not to hate her as I had come to hate her over the years... And I wanted, too, to apologise for my weakness.

"Dad?"

I smiled. "Come on," I said. "How about lunch at the Blue Man? We have a lot to talk about."

Hand in hand we left the cottage.

SELEEMA AND THE SPHERETRIX

I was in the Procyon III glasshouse when Lady Cecelia arrived. I saw her bulk through the hexagonal pane, her stately deportment tugged out of true by the distorting lenses of so many condensation droplets.

Cycling myself through the air-lock, I discarded my oxygen mask and put my hair in order. Seleema would have accused me of toadying – and I would have answered that I was merely trying to make a living.

Lady Cecelia Ashurst was the local MP for the British Party, which advocated capital punishment, repatriation, an independent biological deterrent and the restitution of the monarchy.

"Lady Cecelia!" I said. "How wonderful to see you."

She was a short, stout woman in her fifties with a round, powdered face – which Seleema said resembled an uncooked chapatti – and a blue-rinsed bee-hive hair-do.

She'd been decidedly patronising when she called in a fortnight ago and discovered that I was cohabiting with Seleema – who'd gone out of her way to make the fact obvious.

"Mr Mitchell," Lady Cecelia said now. "You have the plant?"

"I picked it up from Leeds' spaceport last week. It's coming along fine." I'd transported it home in a carricase filled with an analogue of the atmosphere of Procyon III. Seleema had turned her pretty nose up at the growth, which resembled a big, putrescent artichoke.

Lady Cecelia asked, "I wonder if I might take a little peek?"

"Certainly. If you'd care to step inside…"

"In there?" She regarded the glasshouse, a diaphanous dome full of swirling gasses, as if it were a torture chamber.

(Seleema had commented, on seeing her Ladyship's aversion to the planetary domes a fortnight ago: "Silly bitch. Doesn't she realise that there will always be a corner of England forever alien?")

"There's a mask in the air-lock," I explained.

Reluctantly she agreed to accompany me. Suitably equipped, we stepped inside. A blue-grey fug swirled around us. I took her elbow and steered her down the aisle between rows of carnivorous Procyon swamp vines, their vegetable mouths snapping at us as we passed.

We arrived at the spheretrix. Bright halogen lamps illuminated the repugnant-looking plant, bedded in a rich loam of rotted Procyon gerbils and volcanic ash. It had grown at an alarming rate and was now the size of a dustbin.

Lady Cecelia shook her head. "I can't for the life of me guess what he wants with it."

"Who?" I asked.

"Haven't I told you?"

She had told me nothing, other than that she was importing a plant from Procyon III.

She squared her shoulders with pride. "I am entertaining the famous Procyon artist Ruvan-Suix at the castle for the weekend. He requested that I obtain a spheretrix for him. He will be performing one of his exhibitions on Saturday evening, and the BBC will be covering the event."

I regarded the plant. "Perhaps it's a gastronomic delicacy?" I suggested.

Lady Cecelia chose to ignore the remark. "Well, I'm glad that everything seems to be in order, Mr Mitchell. I think I've seen enough."

I escorted her from the dome to the parking lot, praying that Seleema wouldn't show up and start a scene.

Her Ladyship turned to me beside her chauffeur-driven Rolls. "I wonder if you would be kind enough to deliver it to the castle tomorrow evening? We're travelling over to Leeds in the morning, to greet Mr Ruvan-Suix personally. The show is scheduled to start at eight."

"I'll bring it over around seven," I promised.

Her Ladyship climbed into the Rolls, then waved a regal hand as the car lifted on a cushion of air, turned on its axis and wafted off down the lane.

I should have known that Argus-eyed Seleema wouldn't miss a trick.

She rode up behind me on her tricycle, pulling a trailer stacked with forks and hoes. Standing on the pedals, she yanked on the handle-bars and whacked my leg with the front wheel.

"Mitch!" she said in a voice like thunder. "Was that who I think it was?"

I stared at her. "Thank God she didn't see you like that!"

Seleema was wearing pair of yellow flip-flops and a purple bikini which, along with blusher and eye-shadow of the same hue, went well against her mocha complexion.

She leaned forward and made a small fist under my chin. "See this? Warning. She comes here again and I'll biff her a good one."

"She's a customer, Seleema."

"And you know what I think about that!"

Running the width of Seleema's belly, just below her navel, was a stitched scar where two years ago a bunch of BP thugs had sliced her with a Stanley knife.

"If we were to do without the custom of every racist in Yorkshire we'd soon be out of business," I said. "Then how would I pay for all your hobbies? Your chemistry, your bonsai and tropical fish, your astronomy?"

She sat down, deflated, on the padded seat of the tricycle. "Anyway, what did she want?"

I told Seleema about the alien artist visiting the castle that weekend.

"An alien?" She perked up. "That's interesting. Anyway..." She looked at me slyly. "I've just finished work. I was wondering if..."

I grinned like a teenager. "Yes?"

She thumbed at the trailer. "Climb aboard."

I settled myself between the forks and hoes, and Seleema blew out her cheeks as she stood on the pedals. A minute later we stopped outside the house.

She looked over her shoulder. "Now climb out and lift me down."

I did so. "And now?"

"Carry me into the house."

"Like this?"

"Very good. Take me into the bedroom, lay me on the bed, and undress me slowly."

"That shouldn't take too long."

"And then no more instructions. Think you'll be able to manage after that, Mitch?"

I carried her into the bedroom. Seconds later I had fulfilled Seleema's demands and was embarking upon my own initiatives when the wall-screen chimed.

"Dammit!"

Seleema lay back on the bed, her hands behind her head, and smirked at me. "Well, aren't you going to answer it?"

"Not with you like that!" I tossed a sheet at her and crossed to the screen. I accepted the call and interposed myself between the caller and the bed.

"Tidings, Andrew." Grant Carson smiled out at me. "How's life?"

"Couldn't be better. Business or pleasure, Grant?"

Carson was the North of England reporter for the BBC. We'd met when he covered the opening of my nursery five years ago, the first of its kind in Europe.

"Business, I'm afraid. I'll be over your way tomorrow to cover the British Party pow-wow at Ashurst Castle. Lady Ashurst is getting together a few big guns – cabinet ministers, film stars... There'll even be a few church-men and women, as well as the usual heads of the pro-life brigade and assorted crackpots. It's a fund-raising event for the forthcoming elections."

He stared past me and squinted at Seleema. "Did you happen to know that you're quite naked, my dear?"

"Mitch was about to have his wanton way." She smiled at him, sweetly.

"Evidently," Grant said, and managed to drag his gaze back to me. "Andrew, I've heard a rumour that her Ladyship has hired an alien artist to do a turn. Any idea what that's all about?"

I told him about the alien called Ruvan-Suix, and that he hailed from Procyon III.

"But is it true that you're growing some kind of extraterrestrial vegetable for this alien?"

I smiled. "How did you find that out?"

"Have my contacts," he said. "Any idea what the alien will do with it?"

"I'm not at all sure, Grant. But I have a feeling that it might be something mundane such as eat it."

Grant pursed his lips. "Hokay. Oh, well. Are you going to the do tomorrow?"

"Delivering the spheretrix around seven. I don't think I'll be staying for the show. Seleema won't let me."

She looked up from examining her purple toe-nails. "Lady C and I hold diametrically opposed and categorically irreconcilable opinions," she said. "And I wouldn't be seen dead at the castle."

Grant raised an invisible glass. "Admirable sentiments, my dear."

He leaned forward and whispered, "Jesus, Andrew. What does such a vision of loveliness see in a drunken old slob like you?"

"Charm," I began. "Wit, wisdom..."

"Enough. Catch you tomorrow. Adios, Seleema." He cut the connection.

"Now," Seleema said, "where were we...?"

Later I showered while Seleema sat at her computer and busied herself with the internet. I returned to the bed and lay down with my first scotch of the evening, watching Seleema as she tapped away. I'd become accustomed to her beauty over the years, but I found her mannerisms and gestures ever fascinating: the way she nipped her tongue between her teeth in concentration, or trawled the back of her hand unselfconsciously across her sniffling nose...

As I gazed at her now, I considered what Grant had said.

What did the young, attractive and unique Seleema see in me, I wondered? She'd run away from home a couple of years ago, and applied for work at the nursery soon after. I hired her because she told me in the interview that her favourite books were *Nausea* and Tintin, and not because she was young and pretty. But it wasn't long before I fell head over heels... I liked to think that Seleema loved me, too. I might have been forty, running to fat and, the truth to tell, a bit thick, but I was also the only source of affection and stability in a world she viewed as hostile.

I nodded off, and woke a short time later. She turned to me and said, "Mitch, look."

She indicated the screen, but I was too tired to concentrate.

"It's about the Procyon artist," she said.

"Mmm," I mumbled, burying my head in the pillow.

"How interesting…" she said, but I was drifting off again.

The following day was another scorcher, nudging one hundred. Around midday I was in the Antares glasshouse when a knock sounded on the glass. Seleema peered in at me, gesturing towards the car-park.

I stepped through the air-lock.

Today she was wearing a lilac shalwar kameez and a pair of muddy wellington boots. "You have a visitor."

"Don't tell me," I said. "Her Ladyship?"

"She's in the car-park."

Lady Cecelia's Rolls Royce stood among the smaller vehicles like a whale among minnows. As we approached, her Ladyship climbed out. "Mr Mitchell." She looked Seleema up and down. "Miss Mohammed, you're actually wearing clothes today."

Seleema gave her a dazzling smile, challenging in its exaggeration, but said nothing.

"Lady Cecelia, what can I do for you?" I said.

"I trust you're not *too* busy, Mr Mitchell?" she said, glancing around at the milling visitors making their way towards the domes. She appeared uncomfortable. "I have a small request to make."

Seleema shot off another big smile. "Oh, I'm sure Mitch will be *most* accommodating, won't you, Mitch?"

Lady Cecelia looked unsurely from the diminutive brown-skinned girl to me.

"How can I help?" I asked.

"Well," she said, "we collected Mr Ruvan-Suix from the spaceport, and on the way back he complained of feeling a little under the weather. He wondered if it might be possible for us to make a slight detour to take in your nursery. He would like to immerse himself in the atmosphere of your Procyon dome for a brief spell."

"Er, yes. Well, why not?" I was intrigued at the thought of meeting the alien face to face.

"Excellent," Lady Cecelia said, waving imperiously towards the Rolls. The chauffeur climbed out, walked around the car and opened a rear door.

The alien emerged, and then I understood the reason for Lady Cecelia's discomfort.

The alien was a six-foot tall humanoid, smartly dressed in a grey silk suit – and black.

I wondered what her constituents and party members might think of her – she who had spoken up for mandatory repatriation – when they saw her in the company of this 'African'?

I could well imagine her protestations: "Oh, he isn't really, African, my dear – he's an alien, you know."

She made the introductions, and Mr Ruvan-Suix smiled and extended a hand in greeting, obviously rehearsed. "I am honoured to meet you, Mr Andrew Mitchell, Miss Seleema Mohammed. I apologise for the imposition. I can breathe the air of Earth, though it does leave me feeling a little dizzy."

"If you'd care to come this way," I said, indicating the Procyon dome.

Lady Cecelia smiled. "If it's all the same, I'll remain in the car," she said, and effected her escape.

"I am most pleased to meet a person with brown-coloured skin," Mr Ruvan-Suix said to Seleema as we approached the dome. "I wonder..."

"Yes?" Seleema said.

"Lady Cecelia Ashurst seemed rather... discommoded when she made my acquaintance. I noticed that the majority of the people I have seen on my way here happen to be white-coloured, like yourself, Mr Andrew Mitchell."

Seleema said, "Lady C belongs to a political party which is prejudiced against people because of the colour of their skin."

Ruvan-Suix's big eyes swivelled from Seleema to me. "She is? Oh, then I seem to have made a big mistake."

I looked at him. "Mistake?" I echoed.

Before he could enlighten me, we came to the air-lock and I cycled us through. Seleema and I donned our oxygen masks, while Ruvan-Suix stood on the threshold and breathed deeply of his homeplanet's simulated atmosphere.

"Truly marvellous," he pronounced. "You have created here a wonderful reproduction of the steam-swamps of the southern continent. I congratulate you."

It was the first time I had played host to an alien, and I was delighted by his approval.

"Now," he said, "I wonder if you would kindly assist me from this suit. If, that is, I will not be offending propriety?"

"Er..." I began, my voice muffled by the mask. I looked at his impeccable three-piece suit, and then through the glass, hoping that passers-by might not witness the imminent disrobing.

"Here," Seleema said, stepping forward. "I'll help."

"On the back of my neck you will find a large metallic tag. If you take hold of it and pull it down carefully..."

I stared as Seleema stood on tip-toe and fumbled at the alien's neck for the tag. She found it and pulled – and, as I watched, an elliptical hole appeared in the back of the suit.

I have to admit that I backed off a pace as Ruvan-Suix's face suddenly lost its animation: the mouth opened in a big O and the cheeks imploded like a sunken soufflé.

Then the alien slumped to the ground – or rather, the epidermis which the alien had chosen to wear on this world fell in a slack puddle to the floor.

From the back of the suit struggled the real Ruvan-Suix. First his head popped out – green, slimy and vaguely frog-like, followed by four thin arms. Then the alien hauled himself the rest of the way and stood before us on six long, spindly legs.

I glanced at Seleema. Above her oxygen mask, her eyes were laughing at my reaction. "You knew!" I hissed.

"Well, I did try to tell you last night."

Ruvan-Suix's face was featureless, but for the long slit of his mouth, placed centrally. Two green stalks sprouted from his domed head, terminating in bobbing eyes.

He spoke, "It is most pleasing to make your acquaintance in the flesh." One eye-stalk swivelled to regard me, the other Seleema. "You do not consider me too repulsive to behold?"

"Ah... No, of course not," I stammered.

Seleema stepped forward and raised her mask. "I think you're the handsomest thing on six legs," she said, and as if to prove the point she planted a smacker on the creature's domed brow.

"A ritual greeting," I explained hastily. "Perhaps you'd care to look around the rest of the dome?"

We escorted the alien on a tour of the glasshouse, pointing out plants of interest. He moved his six legs with the perambulation of a caterpillar, two by two by two.

We halted by the spheretrix. Ruvan-Suix bent both eye-stalks to regard it. After a minute, afraid I might be interrupting some sacrosanct alien-vegetable communion, I said, "Ah... just what *is* the spheretrix, Mr Ruvan-Suix?"

One eye-stalk turned in my direction. I received the impression that he was viewing me dimly. "Mr Andrew Mitchell," the large mouth enunciated, "the spheretrix, or as we call it on our homeplanet, the shu'tutam, is a facilitator."

"A facilitator?"

The alien bobbed his eyes. "The shu'tutam will be taking part in tonight's performance."

I stared at the alien. "Taking part?"

Ruvan-Suix opened his mouth and ejected a long pink tongue, in a gesture I took to be the Procyonian equivalent of a smile. "All will be revealed this evening," he said. "Now, I wonder if I might have a little time alone with the shu'tutam, so that I might meditate?"

We retreated to the air-lock, from where we watched the strange alien and the vegetable. He leaned over the tuberous growth, his four small hands clutching the plant, his eye-stalks waving in what might have been ecstasy.

Five minutes later he rejoined us. "I am feeling magnificently refreshed and ready for the performance," he informed us. He glanced towards his discarded suit, wallowing forlornly on the floor. "Perhaps, considering my host's somewhat primitive bias against people of colour, I should not provoke her ire by continuing to wear the suit."

Seleema nodded judiciously. "I'll get something to put it in," she said, and fetched a bin-liner.

We passed through the air-lock, Ruvan-Suix clutching the bag in one hand, and made our way back to the car-park.

Visitors stopped and stared, pointing. One small boy even dropped his ice-cream in amazement. We made it to where the Rolls was parked, leaving a trail of stunned and gawping onlookers.

Lady Cecelia extricated her bulk from the vehicle and stared at the de-suited alien, her surprise giving way to an ingratiating smile.

The alien said, "Lady Cecelia Ashurst, you now behold me in my true form."

"And a pleasure it is to see you in the flesh," she responded.

Ruvan-Suix turned to us. "I would be delighted if you would attend tonight's performance."

"We'd love to!" Seleema trilled.

"I am honoured," Ruvan-Suix said, and kissed Seleema, and myself, messily on the forehead.

"A ritual farewell," I explained to a staring Lady Cecelia as the alien scuttled into the Rolls.

She nodded dubiously and joined it.

"Well," I said as we stood watching the car hover off down the lane, "you've changed your tune, my girl."

"Mmm?" She was miles away.

"I thought you wanted nothing to do with Ashurst Castle," I reminded her.

"That was then," she said. "Now... I think tonight might be rather interesting, don't you?"

That evening we transferred the spheretrix from the glasshouse to a large carricase and ferried it over to the castle. Seleema had dressed for the occasion in a short white skirt and a matching halter top. She had piled her lustrous hair high and applied lapis lazuli eye-shadow. She looked stunning.

The castle stood in miles of manicured parkland, and already the great and the good of Yorkshire and beyond were thronging the lawns. Several marquees had been erected, serving food and drink, and white-coated waiters circulated with silver trays.

We carried the spheretrix, in its atmosphere case, onto a big stage on the main lawn and positioned it centrally, as instructed. Then, our part in the business concluded, we grabbed a drink from a passing waiter.

Seleema clutched my hand. "Have you noticed, Mitch," she said in an exaggerated Yorkshire accent, "I'm the only Paki lass here?"

"Shh!" I hissed.

We wandered through the chattering crowd, eliciting several disapproving glances *en passant*. This had the odd effect of making me feel quite proud. Almost everyone present wore red, white and blue BP lapel badges, and union flags hung listlessly from a dozen flag poles. I noticed TV celebrities among the crowd, along with a few MPs, page three girls and big-name sports stars. It was the kind of crowd, irrespective of its political leanings, I would normally have avoided like the plague.

"Mr Mitchell, Seleema..." Lady Cecelia descended upon us through the throng, a champagne glass held high. Her glance raked Seleema, taking in her tightly-bound curves. "All in order, I take it?"

"The spheretrix is positioned and ready," I said.

"Do you know what Mr Ruvan-Suix is going to do with it, your Ladyship?" Seleema asked.

Lady Cecelia said, "He was vague as to the *exact* nature of the show. He did say that it was a Procyon ritual event which will unite everyone present in raptures of good will."

"I can't wait," Seleema said sarcastically.

"Excuse me, but I really *must* circulate." She caught sight of someone across the lawn, waved fingers at them and left us.

A TV crew moved through the gathering, and it wasn't long before Grant caught up with us. "Seleema. Last I heard you said you wouldn't be seen dead at the castle."

She sniffed. "Normally, that's true. But tonight might be a little special."

"Care to be interviewed? I'm sure the British Party rank and file will be delighted."

"Piss off, Grant," Seleema laughed.

"Catch you later, Mitch," Grant said, and led his crew off in search of a fatuous sound-bite from some pompous stuffed shirt.

Minutes later we happened upon Ruvan-Suix. He was holding forth to an ex-footballer and his girlfriend. They were staring at the alien with repelled fascination. I noticed smears of some mucous-like substance on their foreheads and smiled to myself.

"On my homeplanet," the alien said, "the question of aesthetics enters every aspect of daily life. One might say that everyone is an artist."

The footballer said, "You mean, like, everybody paints?"

Ruvan-Suix turned his eye-stalks and registered our approach. "Andrew Mitchell and Seleema Mohammed!" he said. "Greetings."

While the alien slobbered over our foreheads, the footballer and the model took the opportunity and fled.

"Ready for the performance?" Seleema asked.

"I look ahead to the communion with much anticipation."

"I hope you're finding the natives friendly," I said.

He showed his tongue. "I was a little apprehensive about the reaction to my actual physical presence," he said. "So I made sure that my man-suit is on hand in case of emergencies." He waved one of his four hands towards the stage, where I made out the black bin-bag containing his human guise beside the steps.

"And has everyone been friendly?" Seleema asked.

"It is odd," he said, "but my reception as myself – however repulsive I may seem to you – is more amicable than that I received when wearing the man-suit. You humans," he went on, "are an infinitely curious species."

"You can say that again," Seleema chipped in.

"But," Ruvan-Suix said, "I hope my performance will go a little way towards bringing you people... shall I say a little *closer* to each other. By experiencing love in your hearts, then you might extend it to others, irrespective of difference."

Seleema smiled to herself. "Nice thought."

"But now, please excuse me while I prepare myself."

We watched him hurry off through the crowd.

Five minutes later Lady Cecelia took to the stage and gave a speech. It was long, flowery and sick-making. She thanked everyone for attending and went on to declare that what made Britain great, in these post-European Union days, was the stalwart work of everyone present in the areas of business and industry.

She continued for ten minutes, an oratory of Churchillian rhetoric which the crowd lapped up. She gave way, a little reluctantly I felt, to a band of Morris dancers and a folk ensemble.

Fifteen minutes later she took the stage again and cleared her throat. "Ladies and gentlemen..." Her amplified voice boomed from loud-speakers positioned around the lawn. "I am proud to be able to introduce this evening, in a one-off performance, all the way from Procyon III, the one and only Mr Ruvan-Suix..." She moved to a seat at the right-hand side of the stage and settled herself to watch the performance.

A ripple of polite applause spread through the spectators as the six-legged alien took centre stage. He grasped the microphone in two of his tentacles and said, "My delight at being asked to perform the Shu'tutam ceremony, for the first time on Earth, is second only to the joy I dearly hope to bring you worthy onlookers..." He went on, detailing the history of his performance, and then introduced the spheretrix.

I glanced at Seleema, or rather at where she had stood just seconds ago. She was no longer by my side.

"The spheretrix," the alien artist was explaining, "or as it is known in my language, the Shu'tutam, is a sentient organism we Procyonians hold in holy reverence."

A murmur of interest passed through the gathering, and the focus of attention shifted from the speaker to the carricase beside him.

Then I saw Seleema. She was standing on the raised platform which held an array of TV cameras, whispering to Grant Carson and pointing towards the stage. Seconds later he nodded, spoke to his team, and gave the thumbs up to Seleema. She jumped from the platform and vanished into the crowd, and I wondered what she was up to.

I turned back to Ruvan-Suix, who had raised himself to his full height and lifted his arms into the air. Then he opened his mouth wide and gave vent to a sweet, ululating song.

It was beautiful; it was mellifluous and moving, and I wanted to weep. I noticed others around me doing so openly, as the song wove its magical spell in the hearts of the human audience. To stage right, Lady Cecelia was dabbing her eyes with a lace kerchief.

And something else was happening, too.

Beside Ruvan-Suix, the carricase was opening and the spheretrix was climbing out on six spindly legs. It moved across the stage towards the alien, who continued singing, and the crowd watched in fascination.

I stared as the spheretrix seemed to peel open to reveal its pulpy, pink visceral innards. This provoked from Ruvan-Suix what I can only describe as a skittish jig as his voice crescendoed and a tentacle – neither one of his legs nor one of his arms, I am sure (though it was difficult to tell among all those thrashing appendages) – snaked its way towards the split hide of the spheretrix and buried itself inside the sentient vegetable.

The artist throbbed, and his song soared, and our hearts melted... despite the visual spectacle of alien love being played out on stage before us – or, perhaps, because of it.

And then the spheretrix exploded.

Something detonated from its peeled interior, and what looked like a thousand seed pods burst from within it and floated through the air and over the gathering. Ruvan-Suix still sang, his song now taking on the plaintive tenor of a lament.

And, above us, the seed pods burst open and the air was filled with a pink gaseous substance which slowly settled across the crowd as we stared up in amazement, and inhaled. I drew a breath and tasted something at once sweet and spicy.

And as if the wonders we had seen so far were not enough, our souls were suffused with...

What to call it? Rapture? Empathy? Love?

I felt my heart burst, and suddenly I wanted nothing more than to have Seleema in my arms. I felt a sense of ineffable love for the young woman I knew I loved but which knowledge was now confirmed by the unlikeliest of sources, an alien drug from light years away... I wanted to hold Seleema, make love to her, show her that our souls were one and indivisible... Sentimental words, I know; but such was the aphrodisiac power of the Procyonian shu'tutam.

Around me couples were embracing and sobbing and others, without the slightest inhibition, had divested their clothing and were making love on the lawn, and Seleema and I would surely have done the same had she been nearby.

Desperately I scanned the crowd for the object of my love. I looked to the stage, peripherally aware that the alien had ceased singing, that indeed he was nowhere to be seen. Only Lady Cecelia was up there, standing now and gazing around her in the amorous rapture that had overwhelmed us all.

And then I saw Ruvan-Suix; he had resumed his man-suit and was climbing back onto the stage and approaching Lady Cecelia with his arms outstretched... and the audience stared – those not consumed by passion, that is – as did the watching millions in homes across the region.

I saw Grant Carson, speaking into a microphone like a man possessed, while his cameraman zoomed in on what was about to take place.

Lady Cecelia moved across the stage, stretched out her arms and fell into the embrace of the alien in the African man-suit.

And not long after that, with the effects of the alien gas in my system, and the image of her ladyship swooning in the arms of the alien playing in my mind's eye, I slipped into rapturous slumber.

I have no recollection of returning home, though Seleema says she found me zonked out on the lawn and murmuring her name.

The next cogent recollection I have is of Seleema in her pyjamas, sitting next to me in bed and zapping through the TV channels.

She found a news station and I heard Grant Carson's excited babble as he described her Ladyship's amorous fumblings...

A voiceover considered Lady Cecelia's standing in the Party now, and reported that already questions were being asked in the cabinet at her Ladyship's lack of discretion.

Seleema hugged me. "She's old news, Mitch! Her party will drop her like a hot potato."

I stared at the screen. "But," I said, "just how did Ruvan-Suix know that such a display from Cecelia would have this effect?"

Seleema just smirked at me.

I gasped. "You," I said. "You told him what to do, didn't you?"

Her smirk widened. She shook her head. "Nope. I didn't tell him a thing."

"Then how...?"

"Mitch, sometimes you're so thick!" She rolled over, reached under the bed, and dumped a black plastic bin-bag on the duvet.

A deflated rubber hand flopped out.

"What?" I said, my mind in a whirl.

"It was *me* inside the suit, Mitch. I grabbed it, went back stage and pulled it on. I'd read up all about the spheretrix ritual on the 'net, and I knew what I was going to do. So when the pods burst, and everyone went wild, I ignored the terrible urge to run to you and shag you senseless and instead, thinking of my country, I crossed the stage to Lady Cecelia."

I was speechless for about ten seconds, my mouth opening and closing.

"But," I said. "But... I mean... Lady Cecelia – she... she went willingly into your arms."

"Of course, Mitch. That's what gave me the idea in the first place, once I'd read up on the spheretrix. It secretes a substance which enhances an individual's pheromones: Lady C couldn't resist me, even if she was a bit confused by me being in the man-suit!"

"Couldn't resist you?" I began.

"Don't you think I hadn't seen the way the bitch eyed me the other week when I was wearing nothing but my bikini bottoms?"

"Good God, Seleema," I said. "Lady Cecelia's a..." I shook my head.

Seleema snuggled in beside me. The news had switched to a shot showing Mr Ruvan-Suix ascending the steps to a space shuttle, turning at the top and waving farewell.

I said, "Do you know something, I have one regret about tonight – despite how it all turned out."

"What's that?"

"When those pods burst, I wanted nothing more than to... well, you know..."

She grinned. "Me, too, Mitch."

She pulled away and leaned over the bed. When she reappeared again, grinning, she was holding something in her right hand.

It was the size of a conker, with a long string-like tail. "A parting gift from Mr Ruvan-Suix," she said.

Before I could say a word, she pulled the string as if it were a party-popper and a pink, gaseous cloud enveloped us.

"Oh, by Christ, Seleema!" I said, overcome.

Through the swirling fug, I watched her tear off her pyjamas.

"Love you, Mitch!" she cried, and dived at me.

THE ANGELS OF LIFE AND DEATH

In December 2015 I was diagnosed with terminal cancer.

The year had started well. In January I was informed by my agent that a gallery in London was interested in exhibiting a retrospective of my work. In the Summer I fell in love with a wonderful woman. For three months I knew what it was to love and be loved, to have the trust of another human being. In August she returned to her homeland and to her previous lover, and remained with him, even though she claimed to love me. She was bound by ties of loyalty and tradition that no passion could possibly break. I understood that, but the knowledge did not ease my devastation. I wonder if it was during this period of mental and physical low ebb that the cancer saw its opportunity and took hold, clutching onto my liver with the tenacious and irrevocable pincers of the crab after which it is named.

For most of the time we go through life in blithe disregard of the fact that our lives are doomed to end: only when our spans are foreshortened by the sentence of terminal illness are we forced to reassess our lives.

I passed through the phases of anger and fear, and arrived at a calm acceptance of my end. I was given two years to live, and this seemed to me like a stay of execution: I could accomplish much in two years. True, I would rather have lived a further ten, but two years seemed sufficient following my initial fears that I would be dead within three months or less.

I could cope with the fact that I was dying; what concerned me more was the reaction of my family and friends to the news. Over the weeks following the diagnosis, I considered many means of breaking the news: whether it would be best to tell loved ones first, and allow them to inform friends, or make the rounds and impart the tidings to all at once; or whether I should not tell anyone at all for the time being – perhaps in the vain hope of a miracle cure or remission. Only briefly did I contemplate suicide; but this seemed to me a particularly cowardly way to go. It is our duty to come to terms with the fact of our mortality in our own way, but it is as much a duty to allow loved ones also to come to some acceptance of our fate.

In the end, before I could impart the news to my father and sisters, the arrival of the Kallani intervened.

I was in my studio, painting, when the starship arrived over Paris. Mahler's Fifth was cut short by the staid tones of a Radio Three announcer. "We interrupt this broadcast to bring you a newsflash..."

An unidentified vessel, the announcer said, had appeared over the French capital one hour ago. So far, attempts to establish contact with the crew of the vessel had proved unsuccessful. A reporter on the scene then described the ship in full and startling detail.

I hurried into the house and switched on the television. The BBC had a crew on the scene, and I stared in wonder at the starship – for it was obvious, at first glance, that the so-called 'vessel' was not of this Earth.

It was colossal, a bull-nosed behemoth perhaps a kilometre long, its silver tegument running with an iridescent sheen in the light of the winter sun.

All the BBC's scheduled programmes were cancelled. A host of expert scientists were wheeled on to give their opinions, as absolutely nothing proceeded to happen. For a full day the vessel remained incommunicado.

Then, twenty-four hours after the arrival of the starship, the Secretary General of the United Nations addressed the world and announced that there would follow a short broadcast from a spokesperson of the Kallani people.

I watched the broadcast on my portable TV, alone. As I waited in anticipation for the sight of the first alien visitor to planet Earth, it came to me that I had temporarily forgotten about my illness. The advent of the Kallani was of greater import than the insignificance of my death.

And then, suddenly, the being appeared on the screen.

The Kallani were humanoid, if such a term could be used to described beings so familiar and yet so strange. They were humanoid in shape – like the archetypal human form as seen in anatomy books – but they were, too, beings of light. Their anthropoidal forms seemed to contain and circumscribe a dizzy dance of brightness, a dazzling skein of filaments that was at once breathtaking and eerie to behold.

The being, who never introduced itself, then spoke in a hiss like breath passing through wire wool. After reassuring the world that the Kallani had come in peace, the spokesperson then announced *why* its people had made contact.

"We have come to Earth," it said, "to take away your terminally ill."

Thus was the task of imparting my dire news made that much easier. To my loved ones I could temper the fact of my death with the consolation of a tour of the universe.

I had arranged a small party of family and friends, a week before Christmas, to celebrate the success of my London exhibition

I was called upon, in the course of the night, to say a few words. When I had the floor, drink in hand but sober still, I looked around at the smiling faces of friends and loved ones. I had known most of these people all my life. They were expecting a humorous little speech, an anecdote or two, after which they would applaud and raise their glasses to my success.

The pain chose that moment to bite deeper. I tried not to react; I broke into a cold sweat, and said, "Two weeks ago I discovered that I was ill."

I stared around the gathered faces. Silence. My throat ran dry as I fought the pain. My younger sister stared, her eyes huge. "Ben?" she began.

The pain passed. "I was given two years. Then, of course, the aliens arrived – the Angels, as our crass media have christened them."

"Good God!" my father said. "Are you...?"

"In a little under one month," I told him, "I leave with the first batch of the terminally ill."

A hundred questions followed, all of which I had asked myself over the course of the past few days. The day before, after applying for the right to leave at one of the many centres set up around the country, I had the answer to a few: No, the aliens did not have a cure for our various conditions, though we would be administered with palliatives and pain-killers while we were away; and no, they had not said what they wanted with the terminally ill of Earth. After six months on the homeplanet of the Kallani and many other worlds of the galaxy, we would be returned to Earth.

Many of the dying, of course, wanted nothing to do with the aliens' cryptic offer. Conversely, many perfectly fit and healthy human beings were eager to take up this chance of a lifetime, some going to the extreme of contracting incurable illnesses so as to be granted passage.

I told my family and friends that, as an artist and someone incorrigibly curious, it was my duty to find out why the Kallani wanted us.

I had never realised, until that night when my friends and family made it known, quite how loved I had been.

The Departing, as we were called, were besieged by the newspapers and television, all wanting to buy exclusive rights to our stories: I spoke to no one and sold nothing. I did not want the unique experience of a lifetime traduced by the sensationalism of the tabloids. I left England without fanfare from Leeds-Bradford airport and arrived in Orly at midday. From Orly I took a cab to the reception station in the Bois de Boulogne, above which the Kallani ship hung motionless, the latest of the city's tourist attractions beside which the Eiffel tower and the Arc de Triomphe paled into insignificance.

I entered the reception centre, a vast blue and white striped marquee erected especially for the purpose. A dozen UN soldiers and officials stood behind trestle-tables. I took my place in line with perhaps fifty citizens of various nationalities, and went through the bizarre and yet mundane formality of having my passport checked against a roster of names. Only then were we led from the centre by an armed guard, across the deserted park and into the eerie twilight created by the starship.

If I felt any fear at what lay ahead, it cannot have compared to the fear of being told that I was terminally ill. I can honestly say, however, that fear did not cross my mind at that moment: curiosity, certainly, and anticipation, but not fear. Later I wondered how much the Kallani were effecting our responses, even at that early stage.

The UN soldier paused and looked up, and said something in French which I did not catch. At that instant I was bathed in a warm golden light – as cloying and strangely restricting as honey – and I seemed to be falling.

When the light diminished, I found myself standing in a small chamber, bathed in a soft red glow. The chamber contained a narrow couch, and a unit in one corner which I took to be a shower.

There seemed to be no means of entry or exit, no doorway or hatch.

Seconds after my arrival, the being who was to be my constant companion for the duration of the next six months simply stepped through the wall and stood before me.

If the sight of the Kallani spokesperson had been magnificent as witnessed on the dulling medium of television, the splendour of this alien in reality was ineffable.

There and then I fell in love with the creature. I was in no doubt, even then, that it was an effect engineered by the Kallani, but even so I could not deny my feelings, and marvel at the sensation.

The alien stood before me, its human outline circumscribing an interior play of multi-coloured light.

"Please, be seated."

I sat down on the couch, and stared.

"I am Tallibeth," said this creature of light, this Angel. "I am your Guide."

I have been in love, genuinely in love, only once in my life. I knew, then, a selflessness and devotion, a reciprocated trust. I had felt unique and blessed. And yet now I was experiencing the same heady sensations towards this strange being.

I took refuge from the inexplicable in the banal. "When do we leave Earth?" I asked.

In reply, the being gestured towards the walls and floor. They became translucent, and through the floor I saw the city of Paris diminish rapidly beneath me. Earth was falling away like a dropped ball, scintillating against the depths of space.

The walls were still translucent. I stared around at the stars, the moon, the primitive in me afraid. "Where's the ship?" I asked. "How are we travelling?"

I made out the approximation of features on the face of my Kallani guide. The semblance of lips gave a tolerant smile. "We do not need the ship," Tallibeth said. "We travel through space..." it seemed to search for the right word, "that we have... *reduced*. We will arrive in two of your days."

"Arrive," I repeated, "at your homeplanet?"

It inclined its head.

"And then?" I asked.

"And then I will commence my duty as your Guide. I will show you my planet, and many others, and the many races of the universe."

My mind reeled. I was taken by the urge to reach out and draw Tallibeth to me.

"But why?" I asked. "Why us? Why the terminally ill?" I paused, staring into the illuminated face of the Angel. "What do you want from us, in return?"

Tallibeth said, with the sibilance of silk drawn over steel, "That need not concern you," and it was a measure of the control which the Kallani exerted over us that I did not even question the alien's dismissal of my curiosity.

"You must be tired," it said. "Please, lie down and sleep."

It was a only mid-afternoon, and I had awoken late. And yet upon the very suggestion, I did indeed feel tired. I lay down, staring up at the Angel called Tallibeth, my Guide, who stood watch as sleep claimed me.

~

Some time later I half-woke to find myself lying paralysed, staring around at the ceiling and walls, no longer transparent but returned to a soft red glow.

Tallibeth was sitting on the couch beside me, its lower back impinging, indeed melding with, my thigh. As I stared, incredulous, the Angel positioned itself further onto the couch, its midriff commingling with my own, and then pivoted so as to swing itself and lie down on the couch that I occupied. Unable to scream, I watched the creature's lighted spine lower itself towards me, the back of its head approach my face.

Seconds later its form submerged itself within my body, and my vision filled with light, and my head with a sensation of such ineffable union that even human love, the moment of ultimate union at the height of passion, could not match.

Hours seemed to pass. I was strung out on an extended vector of ecstasy. I wished that it would never end; it came to me that this was what existence was all about, that I had been born to participate in this very experience.

Without warning, an untold time later, Tallibeth sat up on the couch, vacating me, diminishing the ecstasy but leaving an after-echo for me to savour. I watched its lambent form part company with me, and it floated, first in a sitting position, and then in a tight foetal ball, through the air, turning like a gymnast in slow motion. As it rolled, its face was revealed to me, and I was shocked at its expression.

The Angel's lips described a tortured rictus of agony.

And, from that moment forward, the pain of my illness was diminished.

We came then to the homeworld of the Kallani.

As befits creatures of light, of pure energy, their world was not as I had expected: a technological wonderland of slick futuristic cities, domed and arching architecture, fabulous modes of locomotion. It was an unspoilt Eden apparently without cities or roads, with few defining features that might have signalled it as a world belonging to a civilised race. Its geography was beauteous and varied: vast valleys and towering massifs, seas like crushed amethyst sluggishly obeying a gravity heavier than that of Earth. Here and there were signs that beings of flesh and blood had once made their mark upon the face of the world. Tallibeth escorted me through sites of antiquity, the outlines of ruined cities which nature had worked over hundreds of thousands of years to erode.

"Once," the Angel explained, as we rested on the bank of a quicksilver, torsioned stream beside the ruins of a metropolis, "we were creatures of flesh and blood like you. We built and expanded and covered the planet with our kind, and then we colonised the closer stars."

"And then?" I asked, biting into a succulent fruit Tallibeth had plucked from a nearby bush.

"Over millions of years we evolved. We became beings of energy."

"So the ship, back on Earth," I said, "and even your...?" I gestured at its body.

The Angel inclined its head. "Forms," it said, "no more. Shapes we adopt to put you at your ease."

"But what are you, in essence?"

"In essence?" it repeated, and suddenly lost its form and shot into the air, a coruscating ball of light, a will-o'-the-wisp dancing high into the stratosphere.

It reappeared by my side, as if by magic.

So the Angel showed me its planet, and more. At night I slept in the open, on soft grass, beneath the stars, and every night Tallibeth joined me, laid its shining shape upon and within my failing, mechanical body of flesh and blood, and we conjoined.

~

Curiously we never in all our time upon the Kallani homeplanet came across another Angel or dying human. It was as if we had the planet to ourselves. It was only one among many of the mysteries about which I failed to question Tallibeth.

One day, as we stood upon a bluff above a vast sun-baked plain, watching a great herd of two-legged beasts like lizards swarm below us, I turned to Tallibeth with a question. The ecstasy of our union still tingled within me, and I thought I was beginning to understand.

"Tallibeth," I said, "are you immortal?"

The Angel turned to me. "We live for so long," it said, "that you could say we are immortal."

I moved away from the alien, as if to communicate my unease.

"Then our union..." I said. "That is what you want from us, am I right? You want the experience of our mortality, and how better to gain that experience than from a member of a poor, benighted flesh-and-blood race who is dying a slow and painful death?"

"In return for the experience of your psychological state," it said, "we bequeath you ecstasy."

"What is it like," I cried, "to enter my head? What's it like to experience my pain, to know that it's something you will never have to undergo?"

Tallibeth approached me, halted. Something in its calm regard spoke of infinite reserves of pity. The Angel reached out, the energy of its hand passing into my chest, and I knew ecstasy once again.

"What is it like," it asked, "to experience my rapture?"

We left the Kallani homeplanet and travelled across the universe, traversing light years in days, visiting star after star around which orbited planets fabulous beyond my dreams.

We beheld primordial life in the hot seas of worlds like Earth in its infancy; we watched barbaric wars fought between races less evolved than humans, and other conflicts between peoples more advanced. We toured two dozen different planets and looked upon as many varied forms of life.

And yet the Kallani appeared to be the only race to have evolved past the stage of physical, flesh and blood beings.

"Evolution," I mused one day as we sat in a desert oasis beneath a fulminating red giant in a galaxy far from Earth. "You seem to have reached as advanced a stage as it's possible to go." I watched Tallibeth, the light of the red giant glowing deep within its body. "What next?"

It turned on me a silent gaze, and I sensed, more than saw, some unspoken sadness.

"When I told you we were immortal..."

I waited. I was aware of wanting to reach out, to effect our union, just as, seemingly millennia ago, I had been as eager with my lover to delight in the pleasures of the flesh. "Yes?"

"Immortality is an impossibility," said the Angel,

I thought about it. "All matter must have some beginning, some end. Even creatures of energy..." I went on, "Entropy. You cannot escape the laws of entropy."

Its lips described a smile, for my benefit. "We live for perhaps a million of your years," Tallibeth said. "And then we fade, we fall to the tyranny of entropy, the heat death of all matter and energy."

I opened my mouth to ask a question that had occurred to me often since my meeting with Tallibeth. At last I said, "You know so much..."

"Yes?"

"After life," I said, "what then? Do we simply... die? Does all we are just dissipate, fade into oblivion?"

"Ben," it said, using my name for the first time, "I'm sorry. There is no afterlife, for any of us. We all live, and die, and cease to exist." It paused, then continued, "So you see, my friend, we are very much alike, you and me."

I stared, appalled, sudden understanding coming to me. "Then the joining, why do you...?"

Tallibeth was shaking its head. "We live for so long," it said, "that we need to remind ourselves of the fact of our own mortality."

I gestured, feebly. "But to live so long, and to know that one day it must end..." The thought was too vast and devastating to fully comprehend.

"But knowledge is preferable to ignorance," Tallibeth said. "And to experience the prospect of death allows us a greater appreciation of being alive." The Angel reached out to me. "For this, my friend, I thank you."

Six months passed in a seeming instant, and then I found myself approaching the time of my return to Earth, to the life which, compared to what I had experienced in the company of Tallibeth, seemed like a dream: my return to Earth, and my death.

We were upon the silver sands of a beach on a planet mere light years from Earth. We had basked for days in the pink light of the primary, discussing everything there was to discuss, the history of the universe, art, life and death... We were no closer to establishing any universal truths; there are no absolutes.

The only certainty was the fact of death.

When it was time to leave this paradise, and return to Earth, Tallibeth approached me and said, "My friend, there is something which I have not told you, which I will now disclose: I can help you."

I stared at this resplendent being, the Angel I loved. "You can?"

"Ben, it is within my power to effect a remission of your condition. You will then enjoy the life-span more in keeping with your kind."

"And you?" I asked.

Tallibeth smiled. "There is nothing that even the Kallani can do to cheat the law of entropy."

"I meant," I said, "if I took up your offer of a cure, would we be able to join in future?"

Tallibeth gestured. "My period as Guide is almost over," it said. "I will soon pass from this tenure... to other modes of being which I cannot begin to describe."

I smiled. "I understand," I said. How could I have presumed that a being of pure energy might gain anything from my company, other than the terrible reminder of its own mortality?

"Tell me when you have come to some decision," the Angel said, and walked away to leave me to my thoughts.

That night we joined for the very last time, and the following day we left for Earth.

I returned home, and resumed my life, and resisted all offers to tell my story – other than through my art. How better to report on my experiences than via the medium I have taken a lifetime to master?

I live and work on the edge of the West Yorkshire moors, in the village where I was born and where I will no doubt die, and I contemplate the many wonders I beheld in the company of Tallibeth.

I often dwell on his offer to save my life, and on my decision.

I contemplate the absolute oblivion to which we are all heading, and the fine irony of having travelled the universe to arrive at the understanding which, six months ago, I was on the verge of discovering for myself: that we are all, ultimately, alone, that the past is irretrievable and the future imponderable, that death is the only certainty and all that is important – and from which we can derive some degree of inner peace – is the miracle of the moment. As daily the cancer grows, gnawing at me with its relentless claws, I know this to be a wonderful truth.

ACKNOWLEDGEMENTS

"Venus Macabre" first published in *Aboriginal SF* (Winter) 1998

"The Frankenberg Process" first published in *Interzone* 171 (September) 2001

"Skyball" first published in *The Edge* 5 (Aug/Sept) 1997

"Bengal Blues" first published in *Death Ray* 20 (August) 2009

"The Nilakantha Scream" first published in *Interzone* 48 (June), 1991

"The Thallian Intervention" first published in *The Edge* (February) 1996

"The Tapestry of Time" first published in *Fantasy Adventures 12* (June) 2006

"The Frozen Woman" first published in *Interzone* 190 (July/Aug) 2003

"Crystals" first published in *New Moon* 2 (January) 1992

"Seleema and the Spheretrix" is original to this collection

"The Angels of Life and Death" first published in *Spectrum SF* 5 (April) 2001

My thanks to the following editors: Charles C. Ryan, David Pringle, Graham Evans, Guy Haley, Philip Harbottle, Trevor Jones, Paul Fraser.

ABOUT THE AUTHOR

Eric Brown has won the British Science Fiction Award twice for his short fiction and has published forty books and over a hundred stories. His latest novels are *The Devil's Nebula* and *Helix Wars*. His work has been translated into sixteen languages and he writes a monthly science fiction review column for the *Guardian*. He lives in Dunbar, East Lothian, with his wife and daughter. His website can be found at: www.ericbrown.co.uk.

ABOUT THE COVER ARTIST

Dominic Harman was born in 1974 and is one of the finest cover artists in the business, with his spectacular art work gracing books from all the major publishers in Britain, Europe and the States. He lives in East Sussex and his website is at: http://bleedingdreams.com/BleedingDreams/.

MORE FROM INFINITY PLUS

Ghostwriting
by Eric Brown
www.infinityplus.co.uk/books/eb/ghostwriting.htm

Over the course of a career spanning twenty five years, Eric Brown has written just a handful of horror and ghost stories – and all of them are collected here.

They range from the gentle, psychological chiller "The House" to the more overtly fantastical horror of "Li Ketsuwan", from the contemporary science fiction of "The Memory of Joy" to the almost-mainstream of "The Man Who Never Read Novels". What they have in common is a concern for character and gripping story-telling.

Ghostwriting is Eric Brown at his humane and compelling best.

"Brown is a terrific storyteller as the present collection effectively proves... All in all an excellent collection of entertaining and well written dark fiction." —*Hellnotes*

"Eric Brown joins the ranks of Graham Joyce, Christopher Priest and Robert Holdstock as a master fabulist" —Paul di Filippo

**For full details of infinity plus books
see www.infinityplus.co.uk/books**

MORE FROM INFINITY PLUS

One More Unfortunate
by Kaitlin Queen
www.infinityplus.co.uk/books/kq/omu.htm

It's the mid-1990s and Nick Redpath has some issues to resolve. Like why he is relentlessly drawn back to a circle of old friends and enemies - and an old love - in his seaside birthplace, the Essex town of Bathside. And why he won't let himself fall in love again. But first he must prove that he didn't murder his old flame, Geraldine Wyse...

Kaitlin Queen is the adult fiction pen-name of a best-selling children's author. Kaitlin also writes for national newspapers and websites. Born in Essex, she moved to Northumberland when she was ten and has lived there ever since. This is her first crime novel for an adult audience.

"There are twists and turns galore before finally the murder is solved... The characterizations are vivid, and in a couple of cases really quite affecting; the taut tale-telling rattles along at good speed; and the solution to the mystery is both startling and satisfying. Recommended." —5* Amazon review

For full details of infinity plus books
see www.infinityplus.co.uk/books

72117486R00133

Made in the USA
Columbia, SC
15 June 2017